THE END

AND OTHER BEGIN

STORIES FROM THE FUTURE

VERONICA
ROTH

ILLUSTRATED BY ASHLEY MACKENZIE

NINGS

HarperCollins *Children's Books*

Books by

VERONICA ROTH

Divergent

Insurgent

Allegiant

Four: A Divergent Collection

Carve the Mark

The Fates Divide

The End and Other Beginnings: Stories from the Future

"Inertia" was previously published in *Summer Days and Summer Nights* in 2017 by St. Martin's Griffin
"Hearken" was previously published in *Shards and Ashes* in 2013 by HarperCollins Publishers
"Vim and Vigor" was previously published in *Three Sides of a Heart* in 2017 by HarperCollins Publishers

First published in the US by Katherine Tegen Books in 2019
Katherine Tegen Books is an imprint of HarperCollins Publishers
Published simultaneously in Great Britain by HarperCollins *Children's Books* in 2019
Published in this edition in 2021
HarperCollins *Children's Books* is a division of HarperCollins*Publishers* Ltd,
HarperCollins Publishers
1 London Bridge Street
London SE1 9GF

The HarperCollins website address is:
www.harpercollins.co.uk
1

ISBN 978-0-00-835584-5

Veronica Roth asserts the moral right to be identified as the author of the work.
A CIP catalogue record for this title is available from the British Library.

Printed and bound in England by CPI Group (UK) Ltd, Croydon CR0 4YY

To the soft-hearted

CONT

ENTS

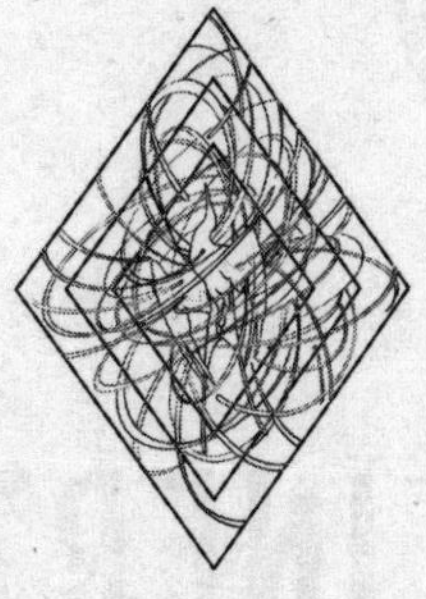

INERTIA

"There must have been some kind of mistake," I said.

My clock—one of the old digitals with the red block numbers—read 2:07 a.m. It was so dark outside I couldn't see the front walk.

"What do you mean?" Mom said absently, as she pulled clothes from my closet. A pair of jeans, T-shirt, sweatshirt, socks, shoes. It was summer, and I had woken to sweat pooling on my stomach, so there was no reason for the sweatshirt, but I didn't mention it to her. I felt like a fish in a tank, blinking slowly at the outsiders peering in.

"A mistake," I said, again in that measured way. Normally I would have felt weird being around Mom in my underwear, but that was what I had been wearing when I fell asleep on top of my summer school homework earlier that night, and Mom seeing the belly button piercing I had given myself the year before was the least of my worries. "Matt hasn't talked to me in months. There's no way he asked for me. He must have been delirious."

The paramedic had recorded the aftermath of the car accident from a camera in her vest. In it, Matthew Hernandez—my former best friend—had, apparently, requested my presence at the last visitation, a rite that had become common practice in cases like these, when hospital analytics suggested a life would end regardless of surgical intervention. They calculated the odds, stabilized the patient as best they could, and summoned the last visitors, one at a time, to connect to the consciousness of the just barely living.

"He didn't just make the request at the accident, Claire, you know that." Mom was trying to sound gentle, I could tell, but everything was coming out clipped. She handed me the T-shirt, skimming the ring through my belly button with her eyes but saying nothing. I pulled the T-shirt over my head, then grabbed the jeans. "Matt is eighteen now."

At eighteen, everyone who wanted to participate in the last visitation program—which was everyone, these days—had to make a will listing their last visitors. I wouldn't do it myself until next spring. Matt was one of the oldest in our class.

"I don't . . ." I put my head in a hand. "I can't . . ."

"You can say no if you want." Mom's hand rested gently on my shoulder.

"No." I ground my head into the heel of my hand. "If it was one of his last wishes . . ."

I stopped talking before I choked.

I didn't want to share a consciousness with Matt. I didn't even want to be in the same room as him. We'd been friends once—the closest kind—but things had changed. And now he wasn't giving me any choice. What was I supposed to do, refuse to honor his will?

"The doctor said to hurry. They do the visitation while they prepare him for surgery, so they only have an hour to give to you and his mother." Mom was crouched in front of me, tying my shoes, the way she had when I was a little kid. She was wearing her silk bathrobe with the flowers stitched into it. It was worn near the elbows and fraying at the cuffs. I had seen that bathrobe every day since Dad gave it to her for Christmas when I was seven.

"Yeah." I understood. Every second was precious, like every drop of water in a drought.

"Are you sure you don't want me to take you?" she said. I was staring at the pink flower near her shoulder; lost, for a second, in the familiar pattern.

"Yeah," I said again. "I'm sure."

I sat on the crinkly paper, tearing it as I shifted back to get more comfortable. This table was not like the others I had sat on, for blood tests and pelvic exams and reflex tests; it was softer, more comfortable. Designed for what I was about to do.

On the way here I had passed nurses in teal scrubs, carrying clipboards. I passed worried families, their hands clutched in front of them, sweaters balled up over their fists to cover themselves. We became protective at the first sign of grief, hunching in, shielding our most vulnerable parts.

I was not one of them. I was not worried or afraid; I was empty. I had glided here like a ghost in a movie, floating.

Dr. Linda Albertson came in with a thermometer and blood pressure monitor in hand, to check my vitals. She gave me a reassuring smile. I wondered if she practiced it in a mirror, her softest eyes and her gentlest grins, so she wouldn't make her patients' grief any worse. Such a careful operation it must have been.

"One hundred fifteen over fifty," she said, after reading my blood pressure. They always said that like you were supposed to know what the numbers meant. And then, like she was reading my mind, she added, "It's a little low. But fine. Have you eaten today?"

I rubbed my eyes with my free hand. "I don't know. I don't—it's the middle of the night."

"Right." Her nails were painted sky blue. She was so proper in her starched white coat, her hair pulled back into a bun, but I couldn't figure out those nails. Every time she moved her hands, they caught my attention. "Well, I'm sure you'll be fine. This is not a particularly taxing procedure." I must have given her a look, because she added, "Physically, I mean."

"So where is he?" I said.

"He's in the next room," Dr. Albertson said. "He's ready for the procedure."

I stared at the wall like I would develop X-ray vision through sheer determination alone. I tried to imagine what Matt looked like, stretched out on a hospital bed with a pale green blanket over his legs. Was he bruised beyond recognition? Or were his injuries the worse kind, the ones that hid under the surface of the skin, giving false hope?

She hooked me up to the monitors like it was a dance, sky-blue fingernails swooping, tapping, pressing. Electrodes touched to my head like a crown, an IV needle gliding into my arm. She was my lady-in-waiting, adorning me for a ball.

"How much do you know about the technology?" Dr. Albertson said. "Some of our older patients need the full orientation, but most of the time our younger ones don't."

"I know we'll be able to revisit memories we both shared, places we both went to, but nowhere else." My toes brushed the cold tile. "And that it'll happen faster than real life."

"That's correct. Your brain will generate half the image, and his will generate the other. The gaps will be filled by the program, which determines—by the electrical feedback in your brain—what best completes the space," she said. "You may have to explain to Matthew what's happening, because you're going before his mother, and the first few minutes can be disorienting. Do you think you can do that?"

"Yeah," I said. "I mean, I won't really have a choice, will I?"

"I guess not, no." Pressed lips. "Lean back, please."

I lay down, shivering in my hospital gown, and the crinkly paper shivered along with me. I closed my eyes. It was only a

half hour. A half hour to give to someone who had once been my best friend.

"Count backward from ten," she said.

Like counting steps in a waltz. I did it in German. I didn't know why.

It wasn't like sleeping—that sinking, heavy feeling. It was like the world disappearing in pieces around me—first sight, then sound, then the touch of the paper and the plush hospital table. I tasted something bitter, like alcohol, and then the world came back again, but not in the right way.

Instead of the exam room, I was standing in a crowd, warm bodies all around me, the pulsing of breaths, eyes guided up to a stage, everyone waiting as the roadies set up for the band. I turned to Matt and grinned, bouncing on my toes to show him how excited I was.

But that was just the memory. I felt that it was wrong before I understood why, sinking back to my heels. My stomach

squeezed as I remembered that this was the last visitation, that I had chosen this memory because it was the first time I felt like we were really friends. That the real, present-day Matthew was *actually* standing in those beat-up sneakers, black hair hanging over his forehead.

His eyes met mine, bewildered and wide. All around us, the crowd was unchanged, and the roadies still screwed the drum set into place and twisted the knobs on the amplifiers.

"Matt," I said, creaky like an old door. "Are you there?"

"Claire," he said.

"Matt, this is a visitation," I said. I couldn't bear to say the word *last* to him. He would know what I meant without it. "We're in our shared memories. Do you . . . understand?"

He looked around, at the girl to his left with the cigarette dangling from her lips, lipstick marking it in places, and the skinny boy in front of him with the too-tight plaid shirt and the patchy facial hair.

"The accident," he said, all dreamy voice and unfocused eyes. "The paramedic kind of reminded me of you."

He reached past the boy to skim the front of the stage with his fingertips, drawing away dust. And he smiled. I didn't usually think this way, but Matt had looked so good that day, his brown skin even darker from a summer in the sun and his smile, by contrast, so bright.

"Are you . . . okay?" I said. For someone who had just found out that he was about to die, he seemed pretty calm.

"I guess," he said. "I'm sure it has more to do with the drug cocktail they have me on than some kind of 'inner peace, surrendering to fate' thing."

He had a point. Dr. Albertson had to have perfected the unique combination of substances that made a dying person calm, capable of appreciating their last visitation, instead of panicking the whole time. But then again, Matt had never reacted to things quite the way I expected him to, so it wouldn't have surprised me to learn that, in the face of death, he was as calm as still water.

He glanced at me. "This is our first Chase Wolcott concert. Right?"

"Yeah," I said. "I know that because the girl next to you is going to give you a cigarette burn at some point."

"Ah yes, she was a gem. Lapis lazuli. Maybe ruby."

"You don't have to *pick* the gem."

"That's what you always say."

My smile fell away. Some habits of friendship were like muscle memory, rising up even when everything else had changed. I knew our jokes, our rhythms, the choreography of our friendship. But that didn't take away what we were now. Any normal person would have been stumbling through their second apology by now, desperate to make things right before our time was over. Any normal person would have been crying, too, at the last sight of him.

Be normal, I told myself, willing the tears to come. *Just now, just for him.*

"Why am I here, Matt?" I said.

Dry eyed.

"You didn't want to see me?" he said.

"It's not that." It wasn't a lie. I both did and didn't want to see him—wanted to, because this was one of the last times I would get to, and didn't want to, because . . . well, because of what I had done to him. Because it hurt too much and I'd never been any good at feeling pain.

"I'm not so sure." He tilted his head. "I want to tell you a story, that's all. And you'll bear with me, because you know this is all the time I get."

"Matt . . ." But there was no point in arguing with him. He was right—this was probably all the time he would get.

"Come on. This isn't where the story starts." He reached for my hand, and the scene changed.

I knew Matt's car by the smell: old crackers and a stale "new-car smell" air freshener, which was dangling from the rearview mirror. My feet crunched receipts and spilled potato chips in the foot well. Unlike new cars, powered by electricity, this one was an old hybrid, so it made a sound somewhere between a whistle and a hum.

The dashboard lit his face blue from beneath, making the whites of his eyes glow. He had driven the others home—all the people from the party who lived in this general area—and saved me for last, because I was closest. He and I had never really spoken before that night, when we had stumbled across each other in a game of strip poker. I had lost a sweater and two socks. He had been on the verge of losing his boxers when he declared that he was about to miss his curfew. How convenient.

Even inside the memory, I blushed, thinking of his bare

skin at the poker table. He'd had the kind of body someone got right after a growth spurt, long and lanky and a little hunched, like he was uncomfortable with how tall he'd gotten.

I picked up one of the receipts from the foot well and pressed it flat against my knee.

"You know Chase Wolcott?" I said. The receipt was for their new album.

"Do I *know* them," he said, glancing at me. "I bought it the day it came out."

"Yeah, well, I preordered it three months in advance."

"But did you buy it on *CD*?"

"No," I admitted. "That's retro hip of you. Should I bow before the One True Fan?"

He laughed. He had a nice laugh, half an octave higher than his deep speaking voice. There was an ease to it that made me comfortable, though I wasn't usually comfortable sitting in cars alone with people I barely knew.

"I will take homage in curtsies only," he said.

He pressed a few buttons on the dashboard and the album came on. The first track, "Traditional Panic," was faster than the rest, a strange blend of handbells and electric guitar. The singer was a woman, a true contralto who sometimes sounded like a man. I had dressed up as her for the last two Halloweens, and no one had ever guessed my costume right.

"What do you think of it? The album, I mean."

"Not my favorite. It's so much more upbeat than their other stuff, it's a little . . . I don't know, like they went too mainstream with it, or something."

"I read this article about the lead guitarist, the one who writes the songs—apparently he's been struggling with depression all his life, and when he wrote this album he was coming out of a really low period. Now he's like . . . really into his wife, and expecting a kid. So now when I listen to it, all I can hear is that he feels better, you know?"

"I've always had trouble connecting to the happy stuff." I drummed my fingers on the dashboard. I was wearing all my rings—one made of rubber bands, one an old mood ring, one made of resin with an ant preserved inside it, and one with spikes across the top. "It just doesn't make me feel as much."

He quirked his eyebrows. "Sadness and anger aren't the only feelings that count as feelings."

"That's not what you said," I said, pulling us out of the memory and back into the visitation. "You just went quiet for a while until you got to my driveway, and then you asked me if I wanted to go to a show with you."

"I just thought you might want to know what I was thinking at that particular moment." He shrugged, his hands resting on the wheel.

"I still don't agree with you about that album."

"Well, how long has it been since you even listened to it?"

I didn't answer at first. I had stopped listening to music altogether a couple months ago, when it started to pierce me right in the chest like a needle. Talk radio, though, I kept going all day, letting the soothing voices yammer in my ears even when I wasn't listening to what they were saying.

"A while," I said.

"Listen to it now, then."

I did, staring out the window at our neighborhood. I lived on the good side and he lived on the bad side, going by the usual definitions. But Matthew's house—small as it was—was always warm, packed full of kitschy objects from his parents' pasts. They had all the clay pots he had made in a childhood pottery class lined up on one of the windowsills, even though they were glazed in garish colors and deeply, deeply lopsided. On the wall above them were his mom's needlepoints, stitched with rhymes about home and blessings and family.

My house—coming up on our right—was stately, spotlights illuminating its white sides, pillars out front like someone was trying to create a miniature Monticello. I remembered, somewhere buried inside the memory, that feeling of dread I had felt as we pulled in the driveway. I hadn't wanted to go in. I didn't want to go in now.

For a while I sat and listened to the second track—"Inertia"—which was one of the only love songs on the album, about inertia carrying the guitarist toward his wife. The first time I'd heard it, I'd thought about how unromantic a sentiment that was—like he had only found her and married her because some outside force hurled him at her and he couldn't stop it. But now I heard in it this sense of propulsion toward a particular goal, like everything in life had buoyed him there. Like even his mistakes, even his darkness, had been taking him toward her.

I blinked tears from my eyes, despite myself.

"What are you trying to do, Matt?" I said.

He lifted a shoulder. "I just want to relive the good times with my best friend."

"Fine," I said. "Then take us to your favorite time."

"You first."

"Fine," I said again. "This is your party, after all."

"And I'll cry if I want to," he crooned, as the car and its cracker smell disappeared.

I had known his name, the way you sometimes knew people's names when they went to school with you, even if you hadn't spoken to them. We had had a class or two together, but never sat next to each other, never had a conversation.

In the space between our memories, I thought of my first sight of him, in the hallway at school, bag slung over one shoulder, hair tickling the corner of his eye. His hair was floppy then, and curling around the ears. His eyes were hazel, stark against his brown skin—they came from his mother, who was German, not his father, who was Mexican—and he had pimples in the middle of each cheek. Now they were acne scars, only visible in bright light, little reminders of when we were greasy and fourteen.

Now, watching him materialize, I wondered how it was that I hadn't been able to see from the very first moment the potential for friendship living inside him, like a little candle flame. He had just been another person to me, for so long. And then he had been the *only* person—the only one who understood me, and then, later, the last one who could stand me. Now no one could. Not even me.

I felt the grains of sand between my toes first—still hot from the day's sun, though it had set hours before—and then I smelled the rich smoke of the bonfire, heard its crackle. Beneath me was rough bark, a log on its side, and next to me, Matt, bongos in his lap.

They weren't his bongos—as far as I knew, Matt didn't own any kind of drum—but he had stolen them from our friend Jack, and now he drumrolled every so often like he was setting someone up for a joke. He had gotten yelled at three times already. Matt had a way of annoying people and amusing them at the same time.

Waves crashed against the rocks to my right, big stones that people sometimes spray-painted with love messages when the tide was low. Some were so worn that only fragments of letters remained. My freshman year of high school I had done an art project on them, documenting each stone and displaying them from newest-looking to oldest. Showing how love faded with time. Or something. I cringed to think of it now, how new I had been, and how impressed with myself.

Across the fire, Jack was strumming a guitar, and Anna—my oldest friend—was singing a dirge version of "Twinkle, Twinkle, Little Star," laughing through most of the words. I was holding a stick I had found in the brush at the edge of the sand. I had stripped it of bark and stuck a marshmallow on it; now that marshmallow was a fireball.

"So your plan is to just waste a perfectly good marshmallow," Matt said to me.

"Well, do *you* know what a marshmallow becomes when you cook it too long?" I said. "No. Because you can never resist them, so you've never let it get that far."

"Some questions about the world don't need to be answered, you know. I'm perfectly content with just eating the toasted marshmallows for the rest of my days."

"This is why you had to drop art."

"Because I'm not curious about charred marshmallows?"

"No." I laughed. "Because you can be perfectly content instead of . . . perpetually unsettled."

He raised his eyebrows. "Are you calling me simpleminded? Like a golden retriever or something?"

"No!" I shook my head. "I mean, for one thing, if you were a dog, you would obviously be a labradoodle—"

"A labradoodle?"

"—and for another, if we were all the same, it would be a boring world."

"I still think you were being a little condescending." He paused, and smiled at me. "I can give it a pass, though, because you're obviously still in your idealistic-adolescent-art-student phase—"

"Hypocrisy!" I cried, pointing at him. "The *definition* of 'condescending' may as well be telling someone they're going through a phase."

Matt's response was to seize the stick from my hand, blow out the flames of the disintegrating marshmallow, and pull it free, tossing it from hand to hand until it cooled. Then he shoved it—charred, but still gooey on the inside—into his mouth.

"Experiment over," he said with a full mouth. "Come on, let's go."

"Go where?"

He didn't answer, just grabbed me by the elbow and steered me away from the bonfire. When we had found the path just before the rocks, he took off running, and I had no choice but to follow him. I chased him up the path, laughing, the warm summer air blowing over my cheeks and through my hair.

Then I remembered.

He was leading us to the dune cliff—a low sand cliff jutting out over the water. It was against beach rules to jump off it, but people did it anyway, mostly people our age who hadn't yet developed that part of the brain that thought about consequences. A gift as well as a curse.

I watched as Matt sprinted off the cliff, flailing in the air for a breathless moment before he hit the water.

I stopped a few feet from the edge. Then I heard him laughing.

"Come on!" he shouted.

I was more comfortable just watching antics like these, turning them into a myth in my mind, a legend. I watched life so that I could find the story inside it—it helped me make sense of things. But sometimes I got tired of my own brain, perpetually unsettled as it was.

This time I didn't just watch. I backed up a few steps, shook out my trembling hands, and burst into a run. I ran straight off the edge of the cliff, shoes and jeans and all.

A heart-stopping moment, weightless and free.

Wind on my ankles, stomach sinking, and then I sliced into the water like a knife. The current wrapped around me. I kicked like a bullfrog, pushing myself to the surface.

"Now that's what I'm talking about," Matt said as I surfaced.

As our eyes met across the water, I remembered where I really was. Lying in a hospital room. Unaware of how much time had actually passed.

"I like this memory, too," he said to me, smiling, this time in the visitation instead of the memory. "Except for the part when I realized my dad's old wallet was in my pocket when I jumped. It was completely ruined."

"Oh, shit," I breathed. "You never said."

He shrugged. "It was just a wallet."

That was a lie, of course. No object that had belonged to Matt's father was "just" something, now that he was gone.

He said, "So this is your favorite memory?"

"It's . . . I . . ." I paused, kicking to keep myself afloat. The water was cool but not cold. "I never would have done something like this without you."

"You know what?" He tilted back, so he was floating. "I wouldn't have done it without you, either."

"It's your turn," I said. "Favorite memory. Go."

"Okay. But don't forget, you asked for this."

I had always thought he was cute—there was no way around it, really, short of covering my eyes every time he was there. Especially after he cut the floppy mess of hair short and you could see his face, strong jaw and all. He had a dimple in his left cheek but not his right one. His smile was crooked. He had long eyelashes.

I might have developed a crush on him, if he hadn't been dating someone when we first became friends. And it seemed like Matt was always dating someone. In fact, I counseled him through exactly three girlfriends in our friendship: the first was Lauren Gallagher, a tiny but demanding gymnast who drove him up the wall; the second, Anna Underhill, my friend from first grade, who didn't have anything in common with him except an infectious laugh; and the third, our mutual acquaintance Tori Slaughter (an unfortunate last name), who got drunk and made out with another guy at a Halloween party shortly after their fifth date. Literally—just two hours after their fifth date, she had another guy's tongue in her mouth. That was the hardest one, because she seemed really sad afterward, so he hadn't been able to stay mad at her, even while he was ending things. Matt never could hang on to anger, even when he had a right to; it slipped away like water in a fist. Unless it had to do with me. He had been angry at me for longer than he was ever angry with a girlfriend.

For my part, I had had a brief interlude with Paul (nickname: Paul the Appalling, courtesy of Matt) involving a few hot make-out sessions on the beach one summer, before I discovered a dried-up-booger collection in the glove box of his car, which effectively killed the mood. Otherwise, I preferred to stay solitary.

Judging by what Anna had told me while they were dating,

girls had trouble getting Matt to stop joking around for more than five seconds at a time, which got annoying when they were trying to get to know him. I had never had that problem.

I heard rain splattering and the jingle of a wind chime—the one hanging next to Matt's front door. My hair was plastered to the side of my face. Before I rang the bell, I raked it back with my fingers and tied it in a knot. It had been long then, but now its weight was unfamiliar. I was used to it tickling my jaw.

He answered the door, so the screen was between us. He was wearing his gym shorts—his name was written on the front of them, right above his knee—and a ragged T-shirt that was a little too small. He had dark circles under his eyes—darker than usual, that is, because Matt always had a sleepy look to his face, like he had just woken up from a nap.

He glanced over his shoulder to the living room, where his mother was sitting on the couch, watching television. He drew the door shut behind him, stepping out onto the porch.

"What is it?" he said, and at the sound of his voice—so hollowed out by grief—I felt a catch in my own throat. In the memory as well as in the visitation. It never got easier to see him this way.

"Can you get away for an hour?" I said.

"I'm sorry, Claire, I'm just . . . not up for hanging out right now."

"Oh, we're not going to hang out. Just humor me, okay?"

"Fine. I'll tell Mom."

A minute later he was in his old flip-flops (taped back

together at the bottom), walking through the rain with me to my car. His gravel driveway was long. In the heat of summer the brush had grown high, crowding the edge, so I had parked on the road.

Matt's house was old and small and musty. He'd had a bedroom once, before his grandmother had to move in, but now he slept on the couch in the living room. Despite how packed in his family was, though, his house was always open to guests, expanding to accommodate whoever wanted to occupy it. His father had referred to me as "daughter" so many times, I had lost track.

His father had died three days before. Yesterday had been the funeral. Matt had helped carry the coffin, wearing an overlarge suit with moth-eaten cuffs that had belonged to his grandfather. I had gone with Anna and Jack and all our other friends, in black pants instead of a dress—I hated dresses—and we had eaten the finger food and told him we were sorry. I had been sweaty the whole time because my pants were made of wool and Matt's house didn't have air-conditioning, and I was pretty sure he could feel it through my shirt when he hugged me.

He had thanked us all for coming, distractedly. His mother had wandered around the whole time with tears in her eyes, like she had forgotten where she was and what she was supposed to do there.

Now, three days later, Matt and I got in the car, soaking my seats with rainwater. In the cupholder were two cups: one with a cherry slushie (mine) and the other with a strawberry milk shake (for him). I didn't mention them, and he didn't ask before he started drinking.

I felt struck, looking back on the memory, by how easy it was to sit in the silence, listening to the pounding rain and the *whoosh-whoosh* of the windshield wipers, without talking about where we were heading or what was going on with either of us. That kind of silence between two people was even rarer than easy conversation. I didn't have it with anyone else.

I navigated the soaked roads slowly, guiding us to the parking lot next to the beach, then I parked. The sky was getting darker, not from the waning of the day but from the worsening storm. I undid my seat belt.

"Claire, I—"

"We don't need to talk," I said, interrupting. "If all you want to do is sit here and finish your milk shake and then go home, that's fine."

He looked down at his lap.

"Okay," he said.

He unbuckled his seat belt, too, and picked up his milk shake. We stared at the water, the waves raging with the storm. Lightning lit up the sky, and I felt the thunder in my chest and vibrating in my seat. I drained the sugar syrup from the slushie, my mouth stained cherry bright.

Lightning struck the water ahead of us, a long bright line from cloud to horizon, and I smiled a little.

Matt's hand crept across the center console, reaching for me, and I grabbed it. I felt a jolt as his skin met mine, and I wasn't sure if I had felt it then, in the memory, or if I was just feeling it now. Wouldn't I have noticed something like that at the time?

His hand trembled as he cried, and I blinked tears from my eyes, too, but I didn't let go. I held him, firm, even as our hands got sweaty, even as the milk shake melted in his lap.

After a while, it occurred to me that this was where the moment had ended—Matt had let go of me, and I had driven him back home. But in the visitation, Matt was holding us here, hands clutched together, warm and strong. I didn't pull away.

He set the milk shake down at his feet and wiped his cheeks with his palm.

"*This* is your favorite memory?" I said quietly.

"You knew exactly what to do," he said just as quietly. "Everyone else just wanted something from me—some kind of reassurance that I was okay, even though I wasn't okay. Or they wanted to make it easier for me, like losing your father is supposed to be easy." He shook his head. "All you wanted was for me to know you were there."

"Well," I said, "I just didn't know what to say."

It was more than that, of course. I hated it when I was upset and people tried to reassure me, like they were stuffing my pain into a little box and handing it back to me like, *See? It's actually not that big a deal.* I hadn't wanted to do that to Matt.

"No one knows what to say," he said. "But they sure are determined to try, aren't they? Goddamn."

Everyone saw Matt a particular way: the guy who gave a drumroll for jokes that weren't jokes, the guy who teased and

poked and prodded until you wanted to throttle him. Always smiling. But I knew a different person. The one who made breakfast for his mother every Saturday, who bickered with me about art and music and meaning. The only person I trusted to tell me when I was being pretentious or naive. I wondered if I was the only one who got to access this part of him. Who got to access the whole of him.

"Now, looking back, this is also one of my least favorite memories." He pulled his hand away, his eyes averted. "Not because it's painful, but because it reminds me that when I was in pain, you knew how to be there for me . . . but when you were in pain, I abandoned you."

I winced at the brutality of the phrase, like he had smacked me.

"You didn't . . ." I started. "I didn't make it easy. I know that."

We fell back into silence. The rain continued to pound, relentless, against the roof of my car. I watched it bounce off the windshield, which had smeared the ocean into an abstract painting, a blur of color.

"I was worried about you," he said. "Instead of getting angry, I should have just told you that."

I tried to say the words I wanted to say: *Don't worry about me. I'm fine.* I wanted to smile through them and touch his arm and make a joke. After all, this was his last visitation. It was about him, not about me; about the last moments that we would likely share with each other, given that he was about to die.

"I'm still worried about you," he said when I didn't answer.

I didn't carry him to this memory; *the* memory. It was weird how much intention mattered with the visitation tech, in this strange space between our two consciousnesses. I had to summon a memory, like pulling up a fishing line, in order to bring us both to it. Otherwise I was alone in my mind, for instants that felt much longer, little half-lifetimes.

After Matt's dad died, there was a wake and a funeral. There were people from Matt's church and from his mother's work who brought over meals; there were group attempts to get him out of his house, involving me and Anna and Jack and a water gun aimed at his living room window. The long, slow process of sorting through his father's possessions and deciding which ones to keep and which ones to give away—I had been at his house for that, as his mother wept into the piles of clothing and Matt and I pretended not to notice. Over time, the pain seemed to dull, and his mother smiled more, and Matt returned to the world, not quite the same as he had been before but steady nonetheless.

And then my mother came back.

I had two mothers: the one who had raised me from childhood, and the one who had left my father without warning when I was five, packing a bag of her things and disappearing with the old Toyota. She had returned when I was fourteen, pudgier and older than she had been when my father last saw her, but otherwise the same.

Dad had insisted that I spend time with her, and she had brought me to her darkroom, an hour from where we lived, to show me photographs she had taken. Mostly they had been of people caught in the middle of expressions or in moments when they didn't think anyone was watching. Sometimes out of focus, but always interesting. She touched their corners in the red-lit room as she told me about each one, her favorites and her least favorites.

I hated myself for liking those photographs. I hated seeing myself in that darkroom, picking the same favorites as her, speaking to her in that secret language of art. But I could not help but love her, like shared genes also meant shared hearts, no point in fighting it.

I saw her a few times, and then one day she was gone again. Again with no warning, again with no good-byes, no forwarding address, no explanations. The darkroom empty, the house rented out to new people. No proof she had ever been there at all.

I had never really had her, so it wasn't fair to think that I had lost her. And my stepmother, who was my *real* mother in all the ways that mattered, was still there, a little aloof, but she loved me. I had no right to feel anything, I told myself, and moreover, I didn't want to.

But still, I retreated deep inside myself, like an animal burrowing underground and curling up for warmth. I started falling asleep in class, falling asleep on top of my homework. Waking in the middle of the night to a gnawing stomach and an irrepressible sob. I stopped going out on Friday nights, and then Saturdays, and then weekdays. The desk I kept reserved strictly for art projects went unused. My mother—stepmother, whatever she was—took me to specialists in chronic fatigue; she had me tested for anemia; she spent hours researching conditions on the internet, until one doctor finally suggested depression. I left the office with a prescription that was supposed to fix everything. But I never filled it.

It was at school, of all places, that Matt and I found our ending. Three months ago. It was only him and me in fifth period lunch, in April, when the air-conditioning was on full blast inside so we sat under an apple tree on the front lawn. I had been going to the library to sleep during our lunch hour for the past few weeks, claiming that I had homework to do, but that day he had insisted that I eat with him.

He tried to speak to me, but I had trouble focusing on what he was saying, so mostly I just chewed. At one point I dropped my orange and it tumbled away from me, settling in the tree roots a few feet away. I reached for it and my sleeve pulled back, revealing a healing wound, sealed but unmistakable. I had dug into myself with a blade to make myself feel *full* of something instead of empty—the rush of adrenaline, of pain, was better than the hollowness. I had looked it up beforehand to figure out how to sterilize the edge, how to know how far to go so I wouldn't puncture something essential. I wanted to know, to have my body *tell* me, that I was still alive.

I didn't bother to explain it away. Matt wasn't an idiot. He wouldn't buy that I had slipped while shaving or something. As if I shaved my arm hair.

"Did you go off the meds?" he said, his tone grave.

"What are you, my dad?" I pulled my sleeve down and

cradled the orange in my lap. "Lay off, Matt."

"Well, did you?"

"No. I didn't go off them. Because I never started taking them."

"What?" He scowled at me. "You have a doctor who tells you that you have a problem, and you don't even try the solution?"

"The doctor wants me to be like everybody else. *I* am not a problem."

"No, you're a kid refusing to take her vitamins," he said, incredulous.

"I don't need to be drugged because I don't act the way other people want me to!"

"People like me?"

I shrugged.

"Oh, so you're saying you feeling like shit all the time is a *choice.*" His face was red. "Forgive me, I didn't realize."

"You think I want to pump my body full of chemicals so I can feel flat all the time?" I snapped. "How am I supposed to be myself when something is altering the chemistry of my brain? How can I make anything, say anything, do anything worthwhile when I'm practically lobotomized?"

"That isn't what—"

"Stop arguing with me like you know something about this. Just because you have this emotional trump card in your back pocket doesn't mean you get to decide everyone else's mental state."

"Emotional *trump card?*" he repeated, eyebrows raised.

"Yeah!" I exclaimed. "How can I possibly have a legitimate

problem when I'm talking to Matt 'My Dad Died' Hernandez?"

It had just . . . come out. I hadn't thought about it.

I knew that Matt's father's death wasn't a tool he used to control other people. I had just wanted to hurt him. It had been a year, but he was still raw with grief, right under the surface, and embarrassed by it. I knew that, too. Between us was the memory of him sobbing in the car while he held tight to my hand.

After weeks of ignoring his texts, and lying to him about why I couldn't come hang out, and snapping at every little thing, I guess me using his dad's death against him was the last straw. Even then, I hadn't blamed him. It was practically a reflex to blame myself anyway.

"Matt," I started to say.

"You know what?" he said, coming to his feet. "Do whatever you want. I'm done here."

"I made a mistake," Matt said, and his mouth was the first thing to materialize in the new memory—the lower lip bigger than the top one, even his speech a little lopsided, favoring the dimpled side. "I should have started the story here."

We were in the art room. It was bright white and always smelled like paint and crayons. There were racks along the back wall, where people put their projects to dry at the end of each class period. Before I had started failing art because I didn't turn in two of my projects, I had come here after school every other day to work. I liked the hum of the lights, the peace of the place. Peace wasn't something that came easily to me.

My classmates were in a half circle in front of me. I was sitting in a chair, a desk to my right, and there were wires stretching from electrodes on my head to a machine beside me. The screen faced my classmates. Even without the electrodes, I knew how old I was by the color of my fingernails—my freshman year of high school, I had been obsessed with painting my nails in increasingly garish and ugly colors, lime green and sparkly purple, glow-in-the-dark blue and burnt orange. I liked to take something that was supposed to be pretty and make it ugly instead. Or interesting. Sometimes I couldn't tell the difference between the two.

This was the second major art project of my freshman year, after the photographs of the love rocks. I had become fascinated by the inside of the brain, like it would give me explanations for everything that had happened to me and everything happening inside me. A strange stroke of inspiration, and I had applied for a young artists' grant to purchase this portable equipment, at the forefront of medical advances in neuroscience. A doctor had taught me how to use it, spending several hours with me after school one day, and I had wheeled it into my art class soon afterward.

I didn't say anything to explain it, just hooked myself up to the machine and showed the class my brain waves and how I could alter them. I did a relaxation exercise first, showing my brain on meditation; then I did math problems.

I listened to one of my favorite comedians. I recounted my most embarrassing memory: sneezing and getting snot all over my face during a school presentation in sixth grade. My brain waves shifted and changed depending on what I was doing.

I kept my brain waves clean of emotional turmoil—the muck of my mother not coming downstairs for breakfast that one morning when I was five, the empty space in the driveway where her car had been. I kept secret the chaos of my heart and guts. I was only interested in showing the mechanics of my mind, like the gears in a clock.

When I finished, the class greeted me with scattered applause. Unenthused, but that wasn't surprising. They never liked anything I did. One of the girls raised her hand and asked our teacher, "Um . . . Mr. Gregory? Does that even count as art? I mean, she just showed us her brain."

"It counts as performance art, Jessa," Mr. Gregory said, taking off his glasses. "Think about what you just said—she *showed us* her *brain*. An act of vulnerability. That is incredibly rare, in life and in art. Art is, above all things, both vulnerable and brave."

He gave me a wink. Mr. Gregory was part of the peace of this room. He always seemed to understand what I was getting at, even if I couldn't quite get myself there.

"Why are we here?" I said to Visitation Matthew, frowning. "We didn't even *know* each other yet."

Matt was sitting near the back of the class, on the side, his head bent over a notebook. He smiled at me within the visitation. Dimpled cheek, crinkled eyes, a flash of white teeth.

"This is where our story started," he said. "You were so . . . I mean, their opinions were completely irrelevant to you. It's like while everyone else was listening to one song, you were listening to another. And God, I loved that. I wanted it for myself."

It made me feel strange—weightless in places, like I was turning into tissue paper and butterfly wings.

"You think I didn't care what they thought of me?" I shook my head. I couldn't let him believe a lie about me, not now. "Of course I cared. I still can't think about it without blushing."

"Fair enough," he said. "But I went to that party sophomore year because I found out you were going and . . . I wanted to get to know you. I loved this project. I loved everything you did in art class. I felt like you had showed yourself to me, and I wanted to return the favor."

My cheeks felt a little warm. "You never said."

"Well, you've said before that talking about old projects embarrasses you," he said, shrugging. "So I never wanted to bring it up."

"*This* is what I was worried about, you know," I said softly. "About the medication. That it would mean I couldn't do this—art—anymore. I mean, feeling things—feeling intense things, sometimes—is part of what drives me to make things."

"You think you can't feel better and do great work at the same time?"

"I don't know." I chewed on my lip. "I'm used to being this way. Volatile. Like a walking ball of nerves. I'm worried that if I get rid of the highs, and even the *lows—especially* the lows—there won't be anything about me that's interesting anymore."

"Claire." He stood, weaving through the chairs, and crouched in front of me, putting his hands on my knees. "That nerve ball isn't you. It's just this thing that lives in your head, telling you lies. If you get rid of it . . . think of what you could do. Think of what you could be."

"But what if . . . what if I go on medication and it makes me into this flat, dull person?" I said, choking a little.

"It's not supposed to do that. But if it does, you'll try something else." His hands squeezed my knees. "And can you really tell me 'flat' is that much different from how you feel now?"

I didn't say anything. Most of the time I was so close to falling into the darkest, emptiest place inside me that I just tried to feel nothing at all. So the only difference between this and some kind of flat, medicated state was that I knew I *could* still go there if I needed to, even if I wouldn't. And that place, I had told myself, was where the real me was. Where the art was, too.

But maybe—maybe that *wasn't* where it was. I was so convinced that changing my brain would take away my art, but maybe it would give me new art. Maybe without the little monster in my mind, I could actually do more, not less. It was probably equally likely. But I believed more in my possible doom than my possible healing.

"It's okay to want to feel better." He touched my hand.

I didn't know why—they were such simple words, but they pierced me the way music did these days. Like a needle in my sternum, penetrating to my heart. I didn't bother to blink away my tears. Instead of pulling myself back from them, back from sensation entirely, I let myself sink into it. I let the pain in.

"But how can I feel better now?" I covered my eyes. "How can I *ever* . . . ever feel better if you die?"

I was sobbing the way he had sobbed in the car with me, holding on to his hands, which were still on top of my legs. He slipped his fingers between mine and squeezed.

"Because," he said. "You just have to."

"Who says?" I demanded, scowling at him. "Who says I have to feel anything?"

"I do. I chose you for one of my last visitors because . . . I wanted one last chance to tell you that you're worth so much more than your pain." He ran his fingers over my bent knuckles. "You can carry all these memories around. They'll last longer than your grief, I promise, and someday you'll be able to think of them and feel like I'm right there with you again."

"You might not be correctly estimating my capacity for grief," I said, laughing through a sob. "Pro-level moper right here."

"Some people might leave you," he said, for once ignoring a joke in favor of something real. "But it doesn't mean you're worth leaving. It doesn't mean that at all."

I didn't quite believe him. But I almost did.

"Don't go," I whispered.

After that, I carried him back to the ocean, the ripples reflecting the moon, where we had treaded water after jumping off the cliff. The water had filled my shoes, which were now heavy on my feet, making it harder to stay afloat.

"You have makeup all over your face," he said, laughing a little. "You look like you got punched in both eyes."

"Yeah, well, your nipples are totally showing through that shirt."

"Claire Lowell, are you checking out my nipples?"

"Always."

We laughed together, the laughs echoing over the water. Then I dove at him, not to dunk him—though he flinched like that's what he expected—but to wrap my arms around his neck. He clutched at me, holding me, arms looped around my back, fingers tight in the bend of my waist.

"I'll miss you," I said, looking down at him. Pressed against him like this, I was paper again, eggshell and sugar glass and autumn leaf. How had I not noticed this feeling the first time through?

It was the most powerful thing I had felt in days, weeks, months.

"It was a good story, right?" he said. "Our story, I mean."

"The best."

He pressed a kiss to my jaw, and with his cheek still against mine he whispered, "You know I love you, right?"

And then he stopped treading water, pulling us down into the waves together.

When I woke in the hospital room, an unfamiliar nurse took the IV needle from my arm and pressed a strip of tape to a cotton ball in the crook of my elbow. Dr. Albertson came in to make sure I had come out of the procedure with my faculties intact. I stared at her blue fingernails to steady myself as she talked, as I talked, another little dance.

The second she said I could go, I did, leaving my useless sweatshirt behind, like Cinderella with her glass slipper. And maybe, I thought, she hadn't left it so the prince would find her . . . but because she was in such a hurry to escape the pain of never getting what she wanted that she didn't care what she lost in the process.

It was almost sunrise when I escaped the hospital, out of a side exit so I wouldn't run into any of Matt's family. I couldn't stand the thought of going home, so instead I drove to the beach and parked in the lot where I had once brought Matt to see the storm. This time, though, I was alone, and I had that strange, breathless feeling in my chest, like I was about to pass out.

My mind had a refrain for moments like these. *Feel nothing,* it said. *Feel nothing and it will be easier that way.*

Burrow down, it said, *and cover yourself in earth. Curl into yourself to stay warm,* it said, *and pretend the rest of the world is not moving. Pretend you are alone, underground, where pain can't reach you.*

Sightless eyes staring into the dark. Heartbeat slowing. A living corpse is better than a dying heart.

The problem with that refrain was that once I had burrowed, I often couldn't find my way out, except on the edge of a razor, which reached into my numbness and brought back sensation.

But it struck me, as I listened to the waves, that I didn't want to feel nothing for Matt. Not even for a little while. He had earned my grief, at least, if that was the only thing I had left to give him.

I stretched out a shaky hand for my car's volume buttons, jabbing at the plus sign until music poured out of the speakers. The right album was cued up, of course, the handbells and electric guitar jarring compared to the soft roar of the ocean.

I rested my head on the steering wheel and listened to "Traditional Panic" as the sun rose.

My cell phone woke me, the ring startling me from sleep. I had fallen asleep sitting up in my car with my head on the steering wheel. The sun was high now, and I was soaked with sweat from the building heat of the day. I glanced at my reflection in the rearview mirror as I answered, and the stitching from the wheel was pressed deep into my forehead. I rubbed it to get rid of the mark.

"What is it, Mom?" I said.

"Are you still at the hospital?"

"No, I fell asleep in the parking lot by the beach."

"Is that sarcasm? I can't tell over the phone."

"No, I'm serious. What's going on?"

"I'm calling to tell you they finished the surgery," she said. "Matt made it through. They're still not sure that he'll wake up, but it's a good first step."

"He . . . what?" I said, squinting into the bright flash of the sun on the ocean. "But the analytics . . ."

"Statistics aren't everything, sweetie. In 'ten to one,' there's always a 'one,' and this time, we got him."

It's a strange thing to be smiling so hard it hurts your face, and sobbing at the same time.

"Are you okay?" Mom said. "You went quiet."

"No," I said. "Not really, no."

No one ever told me how small antidepressants were, so it was kind of a shock when I tipped them into my palm for the first time.

How was I so afraid of such a tiny thing, such a pretty, pale green color? How was I more afraid of that little pill than I was of the sobbing fit that took me to my knees in the shower?

But in his way, he had asked me to try. *Just try.* And he loved me. Maybe he just meant he loved me like a friend, or a brother, or maybe he meant something else. There was no way for me to know. What I did know was that love was a tiny firefly in the distance, blinking on right when I needed it to. Even in his forced sleep, his body broken by the accident and mended by surgery after surgery, he spoke to me.

Just try.

So I did, as we all waited to see if he would ever wake up. I tried just enough to get the chemicals into my mouth. I tried just enough to drive myself to the doctor every week, to force myself not to lie when she asked me how I felt. To eat meals and take showers and endure summer school. To wake myself up after eight hours of sleep instead of letting sleep swallow me for the entire summer.

When I spoke to the doctor about my last visitation, all I could talk about was regret. The last visitation had showed me things I had never noticed before, even though they seemed obvious, looking back. There were things I should have told him in case he didn't wake up. All I could do now was hope that he already knew them.

But he did wake up.

He woke up during the last week of summer, when it was so humid that I changed shirts twice a day just to stay dry. The sun had given me a freckled nose and a perpetual squint. Senior year started next week, but for me, it didn't mean anything without him.

When Matt's mom said it was okay for me to visit, I packed my art box into my car and drove back to the hospital. I parked by the letter *F*, like I always did, so I could remember later. *F* was for my favorite swear.

I carried the box into the building and registered at the front desk, like I was supposed to. The bored woman there printed out an ID sticker for me without even looking up. I stuck it to my shirt, which I had made myself, dripping bleach all over it so it turned reddish orange in places. It was my second attempt. On the first one, I had accidentally bleached the areas right over my breasts, which wasn't a good look.

I walked slowly to Matt's room, trying to steady myself with deep breaths. His mother had given me the number at least four times, as well as two sets of directions that didn't make sense together. I asked at the nurses' station, and she pointed me to the last room on the left.

Dr. Albertson was standing outside one of the other rooms, flipping through a chart. She glanced at me without recognition. She probably met so many people during last visitations that they ran together in her mind. When she turned away, I caught sight of her nails, no longer sky blue but an electric, poison green. Almost the same color that was chipping off my thumbnail. A woman after my own heart.

I entered Matt's room. He was there, lying flat on the bed with his eyes closed. But he was only sleeping, not in a coma, I had been told. He had woken up last week, too disoriented at first for them to be sure he could still function. And then, slowly, he had returned to himself.

Apparently. I would believe it only when I saw it, and maybe not even then.

I set the box down and opened the lid. This particular project had a lot of pieces to it. I took the table where they put his food tray, and the bedside table, and I lined them up side by side. I found a plug for the speakers and the old CD player that I had bought online. It was bright purple and covered with stickers.

Sometime in the middle of this, Matt's eyes opened and shifted to mine. He was slow to turn his head—his spine was still healing from the accident—but he could do it. His fingers twitched. I swallowed a smile and a sob in favor of a neutral expression.

"Claire," he said, and my body thrilled to the sound of my name. He knew me. "I think I had a dream about you. Or maybe a series of dreams, in a very definite order, selected by yours truly . . ."

"Shhh. I'm in the middle of some art."

"Oh," he said. "Forgive me. I'm in the middle of recovering from some death."

"Too soon," I replied.

"Sorry. Coping mechanism."

I sat down next to him and started to unbutton my shirt.

His eyebrows raised. "What are you doing?"

"Multitasking. I have to stick these electrodes on my chest. Remember them?" I held up the electrodes with the wires attached to them. They were the same ones I had used to show the art class my brain waves. "And I also want to stack the odds in my favor."

"Stack the . . . Am I on drugs again?"

"No. If you *were* on drugs, would you be hallucinating me shirtless, though?" I grinned and touched one electrode to the right side of my chest and another one under it. Together they would read my heartbeat.

"No comment," he said. "That's a surprisingly girly bra you're wearing."

It was navy blue, patterned with little white and pink flowers. I had saved it all week for today, even though it was my favorite and I always wanted to wear it first after laundry day.

"Just because I don't like dresses doesn't mean I hate flowers," I replied. "Okay, be quiet."

I turned up the speakers, which were connected directly to the electrodes on my chest. My heartbeat played over them, its pulse even and steady. I breathed deep, through my nose and out my mouth. Then I turned on the CD player and set the track to the second one: "Inertia," by Chase Wolcott.

Inertia
I'm carried in a straight line toward you
A force I can't resist; don't want to resist
Carried straight toward you

The drums pounded out a steady rhythm, the guitars throbbed, driving a tune propulsive and circular. My heartbeat responded accordingly, picking up the longer I listened.

"Your heart," he said. "You like the song now?"

"I told you the meds would mess with my mind," I said softly. "I'm just getting used to them, though, so don't get too excited. I may hate the album again someday."

"The meds," he repeated. "You're on them?"

"Still adjusting the dose, but yes, I'm on them, thanks in part to the encouragement of this guy I know," I said. "So far, side effects include headaches and nausea and a feeling that life might turn out okay after all. That last one is the peskiest."

The dimple appeared in his cheek.

"If you think *this* heartbeat change is cool, I'll show you something even more fascinating." I turned the music off.

"Okay," he said, eyes a little narrowed.

I stood and touched a hand to the bed next to his shoulder. My heartbeat played faster over the speakers. I leaned in close and pressed my lips lightly to his.

His mouth moved against mine, finally responding. His hand lifted to my cheek, brushed my hair back from my face. Found the curve of my neck.

My heart was like a speeding train. That thing inside me—that pulsing organ that said I was alive, I was all right, I was carving a better shape out of my own life—was the soundtrack of our first kiss, and it was much better than any music, no matter how good the band might be.

"Art," I said as we parted, "is both vulnerable and brave."

I sat on the edge of the bed, right next to his hip, careful. His hazel eyes followed my every movement. There wasn't a hint of a smile on his face, in his furrowed brow.

"The last visitation is supposed to give you the chance to say everything you need to, before you lose someone," I said. "But when I drove away from here, thinking you were about to leave me for good, I realized there was one thing I still hadn't said."

I pinched his blanket between my first two fingers, suddenly shy again.

Heartbeat picking up again, faster and faster. "So," he said, quiet. "Say it, then."

"Okay." I cleared my throat. "Okay, I will. I will say it."

He smiled, broad, lopsided. "Claire . . . do you love me?"

"Yeah," I said. "I love you."

He closed his eyes, just for a second, a soft smile forming on his lips.

"The bra is a nice touch," he said, "but you didn't need to stack the odds in your favor." He smiled, if possible, even wider. "Everything has always been carrying me toward you."

I smiled. Reached out with one hand to press play on the CD player. Eased myself next to him on the hospital bed, careful not to hurt him.

He ran his fingers over my hair, drew my lips to his again. Quiet, no need for words, we listened to "Inertia" on repeat.

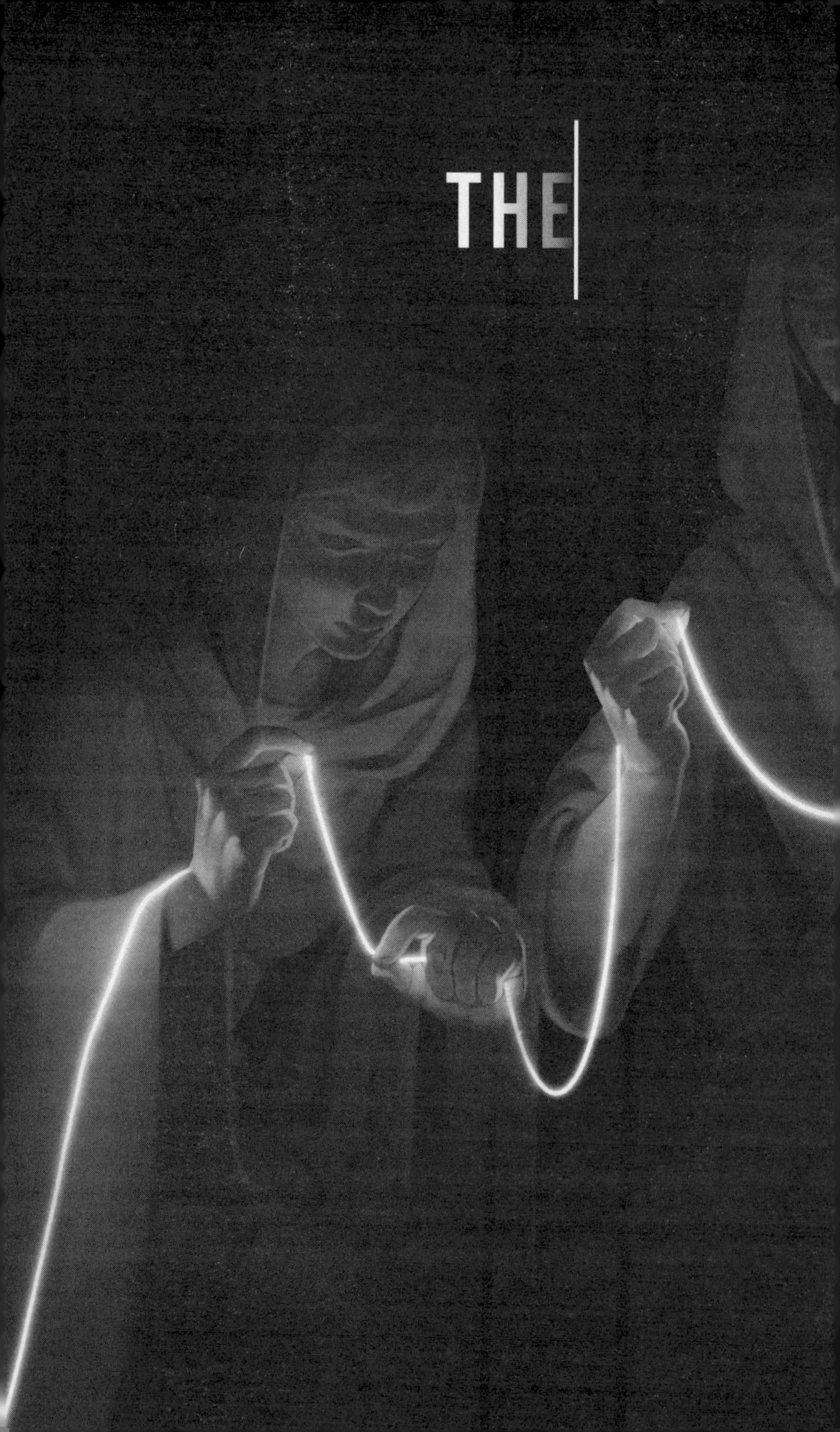
THE

SPINNERS

"I didn't come here to skewer you," she said, low and throaty. "Unless you give me a reason."

She uncurled her fingers so the weapon would retract. It made a *click click click* as all the gears shifted, but she still heard its low hum as she brought her hands up by her ears to show she meant no harm.

She was in a bar. A dirty, hot one that smelled like smoke and sweat. The floor was covered in a layer of stale peanut shells, and every surface she laid a hand on was sticky. She had busted her way in the locked door a minute or two earlier, since it was much too early for the place to be open to customers, just shy of 10:00 a.m.

The only person inside it wasn't human—which wasn't a big deal, unless they were trying to pretend to be one. Right now they were standing behind the bar with a rag in hand, as if it stood a chance against the grime.

"Not afraid of getting skewered by some kid," they said. If she hadn't been who she was, she would have called them an average man, even a boring one. Their face was rough with a salt-and-pepper beard, and there was grease under their—very human-looking—fingernails. But they had all the telltale signs of digital skin: flickering when their eyes moved, a still

chest, and a shifty quality, like they didn't belong in their body.

"That's too bad," she said. "I find a healthy amount of fear improves somebody's likelihood of survival."

Flickering, flickering, as their eyes moved.

"What can we do to improve yours, then?" they said.

She smiled, all teeth. "Why don't you take off your little costume so I can get a good look at you?"

The ET shrugged. Twice. The first time was a human shrug, a *Whatever, if you insist*. The second time was a bigger one, to shuffle off its digital skin.

For a time, as a kid, she'd thought the skin was just a

projection, like a hologram. But Mom had explained that wouldn't work—if it was a bigger creature, it would get itself into trouble that way—knock glasses off countertops, hit its head on doorframes, jab people with a spiked tail, whatever. The digital skin was more like . . . stuffing some of its matter into an alternate dimension. The skin was real, but it also wasn't. The ET was here, but it was also someplace else.

She didn't have to understand the science of it, anyhow. She just had to know what to look for.

The ET burst out of its skin like stuffing coming out of a busted couch cushion. Matter bubbled up from the split, gelatinous and glowing purple-blue. For a second it just looked like a heap of purple crap, but then it started to take shape, a massive torso that oozed into squat legs, a bulging head without a neck to hold it up. And stuck on the front of that head like sequins from a Bedazzler, a dozen shiny black eyes.

The smell hit her next, like a cross between stinkbug and sulfur. It was lucky Atleigh had come across a few purpuramorphs last year, because she knew to keep her face passive. They were harmless unless you commented on or otherwise reacted to their stench. Then things could get ugly.

Well. *Uglier.*

"Thanks for obliging," Atleigh said. "You know, most ETs don't bother to wear a digital skin unless they've got something to hide."

She lowered her weapon, slow, and slid it back into the holster on her belt.

"What is it that you want, kid?" the purpuramorph asked her, in a low rumble, almost subvocal. Purpuramorphs were one of the few offplanet races that didn't need some kind of tech to speak like a human. Their vocal cords—buried somewhere in that purple mush—were actually similar to her own, somehow.

Atleigh took her phone out of her pocket and lit it up. On the screen was a picture of a woman with long hair—the same auburn color as Atleigh's own. She had deep lines in her forehead, and a glint in her murky green eyes, like she was telling you to get to the goddamn point.

"You seen her? She was in here last week sometime."

A dozen glittering eyes swiveled toward the phone, and Atleigh schooled her features into neutrality as a wave of odor washed over her, so pungent it almost made her eyes water.

"And if I have?"

"I just need to know if you spotted her talking to anybody," Atleigh said.

"My customers are guaranteed a certain level of *discretion*," the purpuramorph said. "I can't go violating that just because some little girl asks me to."

Atleigh's smile turned into more of a gritted-teeth situation.

"First of all, I'm a little girl who can make your insides come out of you before you even notice it's happening," she said. "And second, that woman is my mom, and she's dead now, so if you don't tell me who she was talking to, I might do something out of grief that we'll *both* later regret, get me?"

She rested the heel of her hand on the holster at her side.

"So what's it gonna be?" she said. "Carrot, or stick? Because I gotta tell you . . ." She drew the modified gun, hooked her middle finger in the metal loop just under the barrel, and tugged on it so the mechanism extended the needle again. *Click click click.* "I'm pretty fond of the stick, myself."

A couple of minutes later, Atleigh slid into the driver's side of an old green Volvo, patted the urn buckled into the seat next to her, and started the engine. She knew exactly where she was headed next.

Atleigh Kent was a bounty hunter, and her bounty was exclusively leeches.

Not all extraterrestrials were leeches—in fact, 99.9 percent of them weren't. Most of the ETs who settled on Earth were decent enough, and made things more interesting. When Atleigh saw pictures of the way her planet had been when there were only humans on it, she was always struck by how boring it was, all the same texture, like a bowl of plain oatmeal. It was better now, with beings of all shapes and sizes and colors, hearing half a dozen languages burbling or beeping or buzzing when you walked down the street.

She mostly dealt in the ones who had something to hide.

Digital skin was illegal for a reason—mostly people wore it when they were on the run from something. But leeches . . .

Well. Leeches were a different story. They were a predatory race. They attached their silvery, centipede-like bodies to a person's spinal cord and took control of their body and brain. As long as they kept the back of their neck covered, they could pass for human perfectly, absorbing the host body's knowledge and experiences and integrating it into their new, joint self.

Meanwhile, the host suffered in silence, suppressed by the alien until they apparently fizzled out of existence. If the alien was attached too long, and then detached, the person was just a vegetable. Their bodies could go on living, if cared for, but their minds were gone.

All the alien races were vulnerable to leeches, but none more than human beings, their ideal prey. The easiest hosts to suppress, for whatever reason.

It had happened to Atleigh's father. He—well, it hadn't really been him, but they hadn't known that at the time—had lived among them for weeks, dodging their mother and pretending at fatherhood. Then their mom had discovered the thing on their dad's neck, and tried to stab it with a kitchen knife, and he had bailed.

They had gone on the hunt, as a family, the two little girls too young to remember much before the endless road trip their childhood turned into. Their mom had learned everything she could about the thing that had claimed her husband. It had taken her years to find him, in a lonely gas station in

Iowa. Then she had ripped the thing off his spinal cord and gutted it. But their dad never came back to himself.

Atleigh had helped dig his grave, right there on the side of the road, by the mile marker, so they would always know where to find him. And since that day, she had been determined to save the human race, one leech at a time.

Lacey Kent's hand went to her throat, to the buttons that fastened her collar closed. Just checking on them, as she had done a dozen times in the past ten minutes as she waited for the shuttle to reach the station.

There weren't many students on the shuttle from the American Selenic Military Academy, and none that Lacey knew personally. A few teachers—including the famously volatile arachnoid, Mr. Zag—a few parents visiting ailing or troublesome children, a couple of fulguvore emissaries from their home planet, and of course, Lacey herself. She was in her sixth year, a secondary school transfer, so she didn't quite have the posture that the lifers had—she could stand up straight, sure, but when no one was looking, she sagged like an old tree.

"Headed home, Ms. Kent?" Mr. Zag's metallic voice asked. Arachnoids spoke through a complex system of pincer-clicking that no human had yet been able to decipher, so Zag had a voice box hanging from his pedicle. Even though the voice was computer-generated, Lacey thought she could hear some judgment in it. After all, she was going home in the middle of a semester.

“Yes, sir,” Lacey said. “My mother just died.”

“My condolences.” Zag’s pincers were clicking. Lacey had never gotten used to the sound. She hadn’t been in Zag’s class since her first year at the academy, but she still shivered when he spoke to her, the response Pavlovian. “Though perhaps it is some relief that you will not have to tell her—”

“I appreciate the sentiment,” Lacey said, cutting him off. She didn’t want to hear about all the things she wouldn’t have to tell her mother now, because it just reminded her of what she wouldn’t *get* to tell her.

Zag’s multiple eyes blinked at her, but he seemed to get the hint, and fell silent.

Finally the chime went off for docking, and Lacey went to the window to look down at Peoria, Illinois, one of the shuttle’s few stops. Peoria had once been home to a major machinery manufacturer that had later moved to the Chicago area. The population of the city had dwindled almost dangerously until the local government made a bid for one of the space academies. Now, by all accounts, Peoria was booming.

Lacey didn’t care much about the city either way. She wasn’t from there—wasn’t from anywhere, really, unless you counted the back of her mom’s old Jeep. Her official place of birth was a town in Minnesota, and even that was just a word she wrote on official papers, not a place she felt much tied to.

She spotted the wide stretch of the Illinois River, the bridge that spanned across it, and a cluster of low buildings before the shuttle docked at the station. Then she was heaving her bag—packed carefully so nothing would wrinkle—over one shoulder, and walking through the doors to search out her sister.

Atleigh wasn't hard to find. Most families of human military students were downright proper, moneyed, all pressed collar shirts and shoes that made snapping sounds on tile. Atleigh was wearing dusty black boots—one with the laces fraying so the top of the boot was flappy around her calf—blue jeans, and a red plaid shirt over a gray T-shirt with a few holes in it. She had chopped off all her hair, so it was like a boy's, with a wave in the front where it was a little longer. She was pretty without meaning to be, freckled by the sun, and taking too big a bite out of a Snickers bar, so it bulged in her cheek.

Nearby, a pair of uptight-looking primusars draped in diamond necklaces were giving her sideways glances—not subtle when you had stalk eyes that swiveled.

When she spotted Lacey, Atleigh grinned, and pulled herself off the pillar she had been leaning against. The two girls collided somewhere in the space between them, Atleigh's hug "so tight the bears were jealous," as their mom said.

Well, she wouldn't be saying it anymore.

The sudden awareness of what she had lost—what they had both lost—kept hitting Lacey out of nowhere. She'd go along feeling all right, and then open a medicine cabinet and *wham,* her mom's name was on the bottle of painkillers Lacey took for bad cramps sometimes. Or *wham,* she pulled on the black running shoes Mom had bought her for school.

The color of Atleigh's hair, and the creases at the corners of her eyes.

"Wow," Lacey said. And then, to cover it up: "Your hair's gone."

"Yup," Atleigh said. She had swallowed the giant bite of Snickers, somehow. "Supposed to be a hot summer, so I thought I'd get ahead of it."

Knowing Atleigh, that had nothing to do with the decision, but Lacey wasn't going to pry.

"I'd offer to take your bag, but I don't want to let those military school muscles go to waste." Atleigh grinned. "C'mon, let's get going."

"How's the car holding up?"

"Had to sell it."

"What about the Jeep?"

Atleigh snorted. "Not gonna drive that gas guzzler on a perpetual cross-country road trip. It's parked someplace outside Lansing. You can have it when you graduate, if you want it."

Lacey followed Atleigh to a green Volvo with a rusty bumper. She opened the back door to throw her bag inside, and saw the urn buckled into one of the seats.

Wham.

"Time for one last road trip, I guess," Atleigh remarked as she started the engine. And that was all either of them said about the catastrophic emptiness between them.

"We are not having this conversation," Atleigh had said to her mother, a few weeks before her passing.

"Yes, we are," Chloe Kent said with a grave nod. "It doesn't have to be so hard. I want my ashes to be scattered at sea.

There! That's basically the whole conversation."

"No," Atleigh said, pointing a finger at her. "Because you're not gonna die. You'll get old, and there'll be some kind of life-prolonging technology that will keep you going until the two of us are both ready to go. That's how it's gonna work. Hear me?"

Chloe grabbed Atleigh's finger in her fist, and smiled.

They were in an Applebee's, one of the oldest surviving chain restaurants on Earth. A plate of lukewarm mozzarella sticks was between them. The chipper waitress had just come by to make sure they were all right, to which they had both responded, waspishly, at the same moment: "Fine, thanks."

"I don't want tech like that," Chloe said. She wore her hair in a braid that hung over one shoulder. She was old enough to go gray, but she hadn't yet, and maybe she never would—Atleigh was hoping, anyway, because what happened to Chloe always ended up happening to her, in time. "When it's my time to go, I want to go. And I want my girls to learn how to deal with it better than I dealt with losing your dad."

Chloe sucked down the last of her iced tea. Sweetened with half a dozen sugar packets mixed in until they dissolved through the force of Chloe's will alone.

"All right," Atleigh said, a little unsteadily. Her finger was still caught in her mother's hand. "At sea, then."

"And then I want you girls to take a little vacation. At least a couple days. Go sailing."

"Sailing?" Atleigh groaned. "What next, you want us to dress up in preppy polo shirts with the collars popped and scarves in our hair?"

“Absolutely.” Chloe wore her most gleeful smile. “My girls, dressed like proper southern ladies. I’ll laugh at you from the beyond.”

“My hairpin will secretly be a blade,” Atleigh said. “And the popped collar will be hiding an absurdly large throat tattoo.”

“You don’t have a throat tattoo.”

“I’m going to get one when you die, obviously,” Atleigh said. “Absurdly large. A heart with an arrow through it. Maybe some angel wings.”

“Don’t you dare. No daughter of mine would ever get such a cliché tattoo.”

Atleigh smirked.

“Honestly,” Chloe said, turning serious again. “I don’t care what you wear, but go sailing, scatter my ashes, and remember what life is. Two days. Okay? That’s all.”

“Okay,” Atleigh agreed. “But, you know. Try not to die.”

“Deal.” Chloe let go of Atleigh’s finger.

“First stop?” Lacey asked her. She was poking the keychain charm that hung from the rearview mirror. It was cheap metal, that yellow-gold color that shows up exclusively at gas stations and airport kiosks, and depicted the three fates. “Spinners,” Mom had called them, because they were passing thread to each other, one with the spindle, one measuring out the length, and the third cutting it. Birth, life, and death.

It had hung in Mom’s car so long Lacey had stopped noticing it. It looked out of place in Atleigh’s.

“Gotta go through Nashville. I have some things to do there

while we're in the area," Atleigh said.

Lacey narrowed her eyes.

"Nashville is not 'in the area,'" she said. "It's hours out of our way."

"We're gonna have to stay overnight someplace anyway, so does it matter whether it takes us twelve hours or seventeen?" Atleigh said, scowling a little.

"What do you have to do in Nashville that can't wait until after?"

"I don't stop needing cash just because somebody dies, okay?" Atleigh snapped. "I got a job down there. The usual thing. But I can't lose any momentum—not without Mom's help getting work."

"You have to be kidding me," Lacey said. "This isn't just *somebody dying*. This is *Mom*."

"Aw, gee, I sure am glad you reminded me, because otherwise I woulda forgot." Atleigh was leaning hard into the mild accent they had both picked up in childhood. They had spent a lot of time in the rural parts of the Midwest then, and there was a distinct twang there that had proved unshakeable. Atleigh only twanged when she was getting really angry. "I told you, I have to do this. Okay? And since I'm the one driving—"

"It's not like I don't know *how* to drive—"

"And since *this is my car*, which I paid for with my own goddamned money while you were off with a bunch of fancy astronauts at your ritzy space academy—"

"Oh, here we go." Lacey rolled her eyes. "It always comes

back to me going to school. What did you want me to do, stay with you forever, hunting down aliens for cash?"

Atleigh shook her head, and went quiet.

And it was somehow worse, because it meant that she *had* wanted Lacey to stay with her forever, but she just couldn't admit it.

They made it to Nashville that night around eight o'clock, and Atleigh went that whole way without talking to Lacey once. She only broke the silence to ask Lacey if she was hungry, and pulled into a McDonald's. That in itself was a peace offering—McDonald's was Lacey's fast food of choice. Atleigh's was Wendy's.

They sat on the hood of the car to eat, the same way they always did, even in the winter. Atleigh hated the way the tables inside fast food places felt—tacky, like they were never really clean. One time they had wolfed down chicken sandwiches in the middle of an Indiana snowstorm.

"So how many are you up to this year?" Lacey asked. She figured it was a safe question. Atleigh was always ready to talk about leeches.

"Ten," Atleigh said. She stuffed a few fries in her mouth at once.

"Solo?"

"Yeah."

"Damn. You're a machine."

Atleigh grunted a little, and chewed. Under normal circumstances Lacey would already have been teasing her for rooting around in the fry container like a pig hunting for truffles, but she felt weird doing that now. And not even because of their argument, but because she had left. She had chosen something other than leeches. Other than Atleigh, and Mom, and even Dad. And it just wasn't the same anymore.

"Want me to look up a place for us to stay?"

Atleigh shook her head. "I got us an Airbnb."

"You . . . what?"

"You may not have realized this, Lace," Atleigh said, stuffing her burger wrapper and empty fry container in the McDonald's bag. "But motels . . . are gross."

"Yeah, I know! That's why I always sleep on top of one of my old shirts when we stay in them," Lacey said, hopping down from the hood. "I just didn't think you would plan ahead."

"The name of the place is 'Cozy Country Cottage,' so don't get too excited about it," Atleigh said. She balled up the McDonald's bag and tossed it in a nearby garbage can. "No place with alliteration in the title can possibly be any good."

It *wasn't* a great spot, as it turned out, but Atleigh had stayed in worse. She had slept in the back of the Volvo once when she found a peephole in a motel wall. She had gotten flea bites from unwashed bedsheets, and uncovered bloodstains under motel sofas. So the smaller-and-dingier-than-advertised Cozy Country Cottage wasn't so bad by comparison.

Atleigh told Lacey she was going to a meeting about a bounty, and left her at the cottage to settle in on her own. Then she drove out to the ET hideout that Gelatinous Gary (her nickname for the purpuramorph she had threatened just outside Peoria) had told her about. It was even more innocuous than their usual haunts: an old house-turned-coffee-shop with creaky floors and frilly curtains on the windows.

The young woman who smiled at her from behind the counter was flickering like a candle in the wind. Definitely digital skin, no question. She must have been newly settled, because most of them didn't give it away so easy.

"What can I get for you?" she said.

"I'm looking for a leech who was in here a couple weeks ago," Atleigh said. The young woman looked alarmed.

"Leech?" she said. "What—"

"Listen, *Riley*," Atleigh said, eyeing the woman's name tag. "I'm really tired, and I'm not in the mood for the whole rigamarole. I'm not here to get anyone in trouble, I just want to know about a guy."

Riley looked at her for a few seconds, then the friendly expression she had worn when Atleigh walked in fell away, and she crossed her arms.

"The way Violet talked about you, I thought you'd be bigger," Riley said.

Atleigh registered a moment of shock that Gelatinous Gary was actually named Violet—such a lovely name for such an unlovely thing.

"It's the shoes," Atleigh said dryly. Hidden under the flannel shirt she wore, pressed up against her spine, was the needleknife she would need if things went sour. And, judging by the hard look on Riley's face, that was a distinct possibility. Whatever Riley was under that digital skin, Atleigh was pretty sure it wasn't a purpuramorph.

"What is it you want to know?" Riley said. One of her hands was hidden under the counter. Not a good sign. Atleigh started moving her hand back, casual-like, toward her weapon.

"The leech was attached to the body of a middle-aged gentleman," Atleigh said. "A scout. He goes looking for solid hosts, get it? And the others suck down on who he tells them."

"If I had known someone like that was in here, I would have been legally obligated to report it," Riley said coolly. "So are you accusing me of breaking the law?"

"Sure, but not in a mean way." Atleigh's voice softened. "Because you gotta get by, right? So you'll do what you have to do, even if you don't like it. I understand. I've done a lot of things I don't like, Riley."

"Somehow I doubt that," Riley said, matching Atleigh's soft tone with one of her own. "From the look of you, girl, you've enjoyed every second of what you've done to my kind."

She shrugged off her skin, and what was under it was the exact same—except for the glint of silver at the back of Riley's neck.

Leech.

Atleigh swore, and drew her needleknife. It was like an ice pick, but with a slimmer handle, to accommodate Atleigh's skinny fingers. Mom had gotten it for her two years ago, for her birthday, and she had skewered more than one leech with it without hesitating.

She swung it without hesitating now, her arm curved so she would hit the back of the neck. But Riley was fast, blocking the blow with her forearm and then grabbing at Atleigh's wrist. Her other hand went up to Atleigh's throat, but Atleigh had the presence of mind to block that, so they were clutched together in some kind of two-handed arm-wrestling contest, the countertop between them.

Atleigh knew from the first moment that she wasn't as strong as Riley—that was just something you figured out when you first came to blows with somebody. So after a second of grunting with effort, she decided her best course of action was to run like hell. She let go of Riley's arm and twisted into the thumb part of the leech's grip, so it would break easier.

She got away, but only for a second. Riley hopped over the counter like she did that sort of thing professionally, and grabbed Atleigh by her shirt collar. The shirt ripped, and Atleigh spun around to try with the needleknife again, this time blindly stabbing at whatever flesh was nearest. The needleknife stuck in Riley's wrist, and she yanked it free, watching the blood dance across the leech's arm.

Riley screamed her rage, and punched Atleigh right in the face. Atleigh stumbled back, blinded for a second by pain, and struggled toward the door. But Riley was on top of her again, tackling her so they both fell on the creaky floor. Atleigh elbowed and scratched, mostly hitting nothing, and Riley was on top of her, her arm a bar across Atleigh's throat and her hands grabbing at the needleknife.

Atleigh did the only thing she could think of: she threw the needleknife behind her, so it was out of arm's reach for both of them. Riley let up, and sprung like a cat toward the weapon, giving Atleigh room to run. She made a break for it, eyes on the back door. A couple of steps into her getaway, she felt heat on her side, a cut from the needleknife.

It was good she hadn't told Lacey where she was really going, Atleigh thought. Now Lacey wouldn't have to find her body. Atleigh had found Mom's, and she wouldn't have wished that on anyone.

Only the killing blow didn't come. Atleigh was down, on her hands and knees, clutching at the wound in her side. She turned to see someone else bringing a blade down on Riley's spine, chopping the leech attached to her neck in half. Clean. Nice, sharp knife. Silvery blood oozed from the cleaved thing, and Riley fell.

Standing over the body, wearing all black except for those stupid polka-dot laces he always insisted on, was a young man. Eighteen, or nineteen, maybe. She had asked, once, and he didn't know. His ancestry was at least half Korean—he didn't know how much, either—and he was smirking at her.

Eon was his name.

"Don't give me that look," she said, collapsing to the ground with her hand against her side. Her entire body felt like it was on fire. "I was totally handling it."

"Oh yeah, I can see that," he said. He was cleaning his weapon with a handkerchief. He had an endless supply of handkerchiefs, all of them black cotton. "How's that wound?"

"Shallow," she said. "Her left hook was worse."

He sheathed the blade and bent to pick up her weapon, still half-clutched in Riley's hand.

"You gotta end it," Atleigh said, nodding to Riley. The woman's eyes were still open, her chest still rising and falling. He had killed the leech attached to her body, but he hadn't killed the body. He never did.

"I always want to believe they'll come back," he said, shaking his head. He bent over Riley's host and—shifting so Atleigh would be shielded from the sight—stuck her with the needleknife. Atleigh knew where it went—in the meaty part of the shoulder and down, into the heart.

By the time he turned back to her, the weapon was clean, and his smirk was back.

"So are you stalking me, or what?" Atleigh grunted, panting.

"I followed up on some intel and it led me here, same as you," Eon said. "Fireman, or bridal?"

"What?"

"I'm going to pick you up, and we're going to get the hell out of here before either more leeches or clandestine-government types with debriefing obligations show up," he said. "We can call it in later. So do you want me to pick you up fireman style, or bridal style?"

"I can't actually decide what's more humiliating," she said. She thought of Eon holding her over his shoulder, his hand right at the top of her thigh and his face next to her ass, and cringed.

"Bridal, go for bridal."

The door hit the wall of the Cozy Country Cottage, and Lacey lurched to her feet, grabbed a knife from the butcher block on the counter, and held it at the ready.

"The family resemblance is uncanny," the man holding Atleigh against his chest said, drily. Lacey saw blood streaking her sister's side, and lowered her knife.

"What happened?" she said.

"Got in a fight I couldn't win," Atleigh said. She sounded steady enough. Lacey moved a wilting houseplant off the kitchen island, clearing a space for the man to set Atleigh down. She wasn't eager to search the Airbnb's cupboards for first aid, so she went out to the car instead, casting a backward glance at the man lowering her sister to the countertop.

The first-aid kit was in the trunk, where it always was. Lacey jogged a little to get back to the house faster. The man seemed to know Atleigh—and since when did Atleigh know tall, handsome men?—but it didn't hurt to be careful.

"Lace, this is Eon," Atleigh said when she got back into the kitchen. The man—Eon—was lifting the hem of Atleigh's shirt. And as Lacey watched . . . he *flickered.*

Like he was wearing digital skin.

"Hands off, buddy," Lacey said. "I can take it from here."

She went to the sink and started washing her hands. Eon stepped back, showing his palms.

"What kind of name is Eon?" she said.

"What kind of name is Lacey?" he replied. "Are you a doily?"

Atleigh laughed softly. Lacey wasn't amused. She turned back to Atleigh, who had peeled her blood-soaked tank top away from the wound, showing a pale stretch of side. Eon was arranging the contents of the first-aid kit in order of what Lacey would need: antiseptic and cotton balls, butterfly bandages, gauze, and medical tape.

"Eon was helping Mom out with a case when . . . you know," Atleigh said. "He's in the business."

"Yeah?" Lacey squeezed some antiseptic on a cotton ball. "And why, exactly, is he wearing skin?"

She stuck the cotton ball up against Atleigh's wound, not so gently. Atleigh cursed, and Lacey eased up a little, wiping the scratch clean. It was deep, but not deep enough to need stitches, thank God. Lacey wasn't good at those.

She looked at Atleigh, and then at Eon, eyebrows raised.

"You weren't kidding," Eon said. "She's got good eyes."

"Always has," Atleigh said. "Lace—"

"I like to get to know people before I let them see me naked," Eon said to Lacey, leaning into the counter. "I've known your family for two years, Lacey. You think you're the first one to notice I'm wearing this?"

He had a point, Lacey thought. Mom and Atleigh wouldn't have let him stick around if he was the dangerous kind of ET. She bent down low to apply the butterfly bandage, tugging the two edges of Atleigh's skin together as close as she could manage.

"Sorry," she said.

"No big," he said. "I know it's suspicious behavior."

He was a lot to take in at once. His cheekbones alone were head-turning. And then there were his dark, expressive eyes, and, when he took off his leather jacket . . .

Lacey forced herself to focus on positioning the gauze over the wound. Eon had torn off strips of medical tape and stuck them to the edge of the counter for her to use. He was rummaging in the freezer for some ice.

"I'll get you a shirt," she said to Atleigh.

She went into the bedroom to root around in Atleigh's bag for something clean, and when she turned back, she saw Eon helping Atleigh up, his hand pressing to the small of her back to hold her upright. He held a dish towel full of ice to her cheek, and Atleigh rolled her eyes at him.

The way he looked at her, it was like he didn't care if anyone else in the world existed. But that didn't bother Lacey so much as the way Atleigh looked back—her eyes catching on every movement he made.

"It wasn't just a job, obviously," Atleigh said.

Lacey sat on the couch, her arms folded. Eon was on the floor, cross-legged, his big toe poking out of one of his socks.

The socks had little dinosaurs on them.

"Yeah," Lacey said. "I figured."

"I've been tracking Mom's killer," Atleigh said. "He's a leech scout. I went to ask the woman who runs a skin bar around here about him." A "skin bar" was a place where an ET—or a human, but not many bothered—could buy digital skin without the authorities finding out. "Only I guess I should have known that a woman running a skin bar who knows things about leech scouts would probably be a leech herself."

"And you, what?" Lacey said to Eon. "Just happened to be there?"

"I was finishing the job. Chloe's last job," Eon said. Atleigh couldn't remember when she'd last seen him this casual, sitting around in his dinosaur socks and a T-shirt. She absolutely did not notice how his bicep strained against the fabric of said T-shirt, at all. "Following the same trail Atleigh was, just three minutes later."

"Where were you when she died?" Lacey said, her voice sounding a little thick.

"We got two different locations for where the scout might be," Eon said. "I went with Atleigh to one, and Chloe went alone to the other."

Something gnawed at Atleigh's stomach. She and Eon had gone all cavalier to some pile of rubble in the middle of nowhere, thinking they would take the leech by surprise. And there had been no one there. Nothing.

And if they hadn't split up . . . if they hadn't believed Chloe when she said she could handle it on her own . . .

No woulda-coulda-shouldas, Mom had always said. There was no looking back when you did what they did. It just drove you nuts. That was where the Spinners had come in, because you didn't get to decide to be born, or when, or how long you lived, or when you died. You had to leave that up to the women with the thread.

"You can't think that way," Lacey said. "I wasn't there either, At. And who knows, if you had gone, maybe it'd be your urn in the back seat, and Mom wishing she could unravel time, instead."

"Yeah." Atleigh blinked away tears, and brought the ice up to her cheek again to distract herself. "Well anyway, the trail's gone cold, and I'm not sure we'll ever find that leech asshole."

"Well." Eon picked at the toe of his sock. "*That* trail is cold."

Lacey and Atleigh both stared at him.

"Okay, it's possible I only came to Nashville because I knew *you* would come to Nashville," Eon said to Atleigh. "Really, I was on my way to Durham, and I thought you might want to come along."

"Durham," Atleigh said. "The entire eastern seaboard at his fingertips, and that piece of shit goes to *Durham*?"

"I hear they have good barbecue," Eon said, shrugging.

Atleigh cradled a mug of tea to her chest. It was a cool night, but somehow still muggy, like she was taking a bite of something every time she breathed in. She sat on the front steps, her knees drawn up as close to her chest as the wound in her side would allow.

"Hey," Eon said. He sat down next to her on the step. He had a blanket wrapped around him. "Couldn't sleep?"

"Not really," she said. "Not since Mom."

Her mom had introduced her to him a year ago. It had been winter, so his black coat had been longer, and he had looked like someone out of *The Matrix*, combat boots and all. He had been watching a French cartoon on his laptop, eating Cap'n Crunch out of the box. She had noticed the flickering right away, but Mom said he was all right, so she didn't question him. And he was easy to like, anyway. Teeming over with enthusiasm about every human thing he could get his hands on—not just cartoons, but any TV show he watched, and books, movies, music, art, everything. He got so hooked on *The Bachelor* that year that he cried at the finale. He liked speaking French better than English, he said, because he got to use his nose more. He loved hitting his funny bone. He was so *much* that by the time she heard the story of what he was, it was too hard to tease one thing out of the knot of him that she didn't bother to try.

"Humans have a lot of truly useless sayings about grief," he said. "Something about time healing, and her being in a better place—I find myself cycling through them again and again, in lieu of other words."

"Your people don't have anything to say about grief?" she said.

"Depends on which bodies we've joined with," he said. "We don't always have verbal language. But here?" He shook his head. "No, we don't have words."

"I didn't mean to put you in a weird spot with my sister," Atleigh said. "I wasn't sure how to handle it when she asked you what you were."

Eon shrugged. "We don't have time to waste on that particular story right now."

"Yeah." Atleigh set her mug aside. "You handled it well, though."

"Atleigh," he said softly.

Something about his tone made her look at him—and really look at him, without a joke at the ready, without her eyes skipping around his face searching for some easier place to land.

Then he shrugged, and the skin fell away. Beneath it he was the same—focused brown eyes, stick-out ears, full mouth, Adam's apple that bobbed when he was nervous. But glinting at the back of his neck was his other body, the silver streak of the leech.

He was not stifling a human host. Her mother had assured her of that, and so had he. His kind was at war with itself over the planet Earth and its inhabitants—some believed in taking what they could find, that other beings were prey and subsuming their consciousnesses was nothing. And some believed that the only body that ought to be occupied was one that had already lost its host. The boy who had been in Eon's body, once, was named Danny. Daniel Goo, on life support in a hospital in New York City, no brain waves, just a beating heart in a body.

She tilted her head, trying to get a better look. He bent his head forward, so she could see the silver in the moonlight. The leech's body was narrow, about the length of her hand, and pressed against the back of his neck—but it didn't look like it was clinging to his skin, it looked like it had grown *into* his skin. Small tendrils stretched up, under his hairline and into his skull, and down, under the collar of his shirt where she couldn't see what became of them. But she knew they were wrapped around his spinal cord, binding the two bodies together irrevocably.

"Do you feel it?" she said.

"The way you feel your arm in its socket, maybe," he said.

She lifted her hand, and it quivered like a flame in the wind. She had been killing leeches her entire life. Even now, her instincts told her to do it, to cut this thing free of its human host. But no, she told herself—this was Eon. She touched the back of his neck, running her fingers over the silver streak there. It felt hard and smooth, like a shell. His breaths pulsed out, and he closed his eyes.

"Do you have a name for your own kind, at least?" she said softly. "A better one than 'leech,' I mean."

She took her hand away, and he looked at her again, intently, as he always did, like she warranted every ounce of his attention.

"Symbios," he replied. "We call ourselves 'symbios.'"

"Nice word," she said. She was breathless. She licked her lips. "I'm gonna do something stupid."

Atleigh kissed him softly. And it was the breaking of a dam, the bursting of a bubble—whatever thin skin had kept them

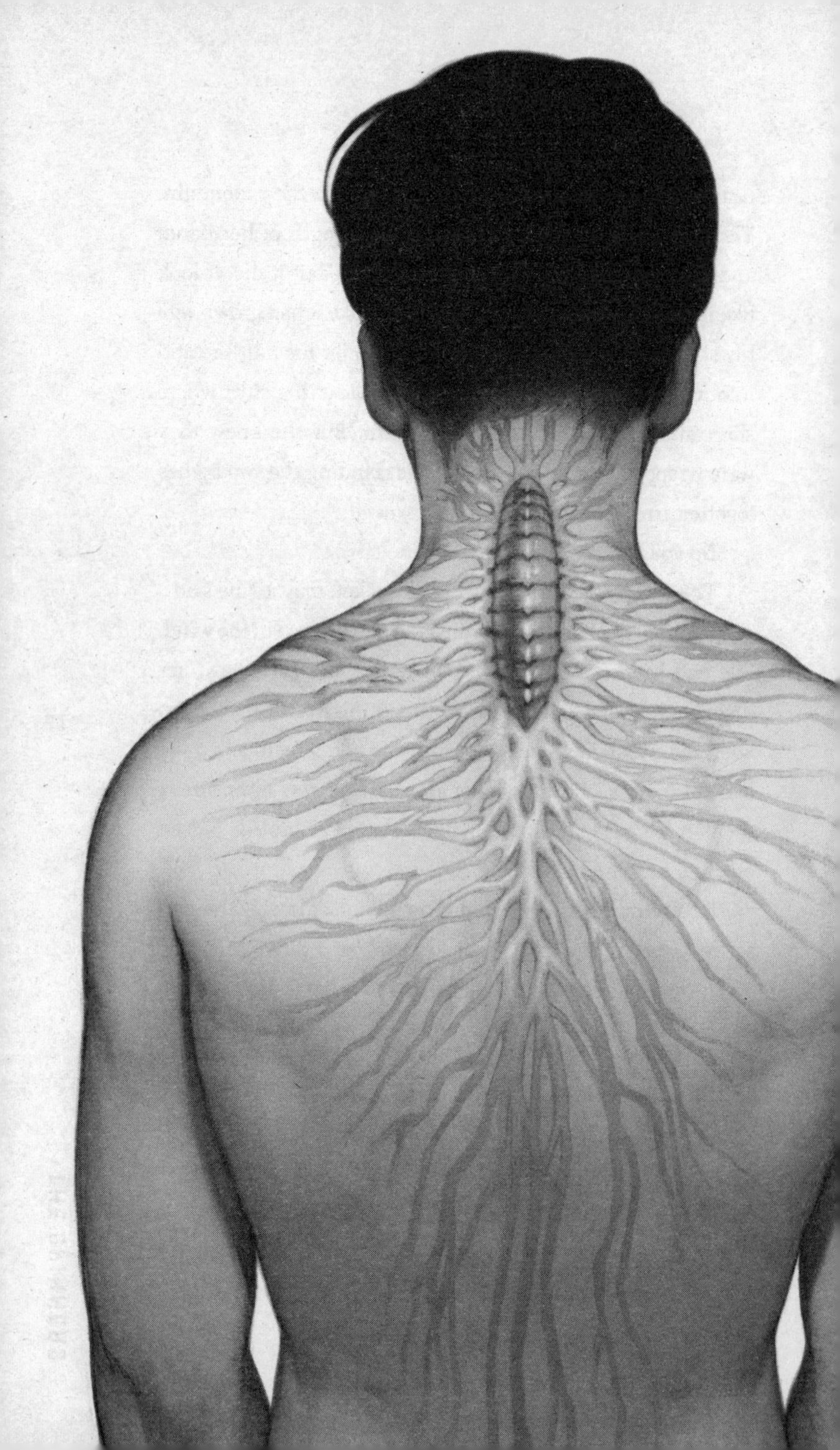

contained, ripped apart. He buried his hands in her hair, his mouth opening, and she let herself touch him, put her hands on his arms, his chest. As good as she imagined; no, better, warmer, kinder—

"Get away from her," a cold, hard voice said from the doorway.

They broke apart. Lacey stood behind them in her school-issued pajamas—which were plain gray, of course, with black stripes at the seams—and a needleknife in her hand. She was staring at the silver on the back of Eon's neck.

"Lace," Atleigh said. She stood so Eon was behind her, blocking him.

"If you say 'It's not what you think,' I will punch you," Lacey said, her voice trembling. "He's a leech, and you're making out with him."

"It's different. There's nobody else in there, just him," Atleigh said.

"I don't *care*," Lacey said. "You make me feel terrible about leaving you, when *this* is what you've been doing without me? Cozying up to one of *them*?"

"I haven't 'been doing' this; this is the first—" Atleigh scowled. "You know what? Yeah, I kept living my life, and you weren't there, so don't charge in with your judgment now, because it's a little late!"

"Yeah? Well I may have left so I could make something more of my life than this shitty perpetual road trip," Lacey said, eyes narrowed. "But at least I didn't betray everything that we are by sucking face with a goddamn parasite!"

Atleigh felt heavy, suddenly, and so tired she could hardly stand upright.

"If something more than this shitty road trip is what you want, then you'd better get back to school, don't you think?" she said. She brushed past Lacey on her way into the house, and grabbed the car keys, which she then thrust into her sister's hands.

"Eon's got a car, we'll take care of the leech scout," she said. "Just park the Volvo at the Peoria station. Leave the keys in it, nobody'll steal it."

"Fine," Lacey said. Her eyes filled with tears. "Good."

All the heat had gone out of them at once, it seemed like. Lacey pocketed the keys and started packing up her things. Eon stayed in the kitchen, with Atleigh's empty mug, not looking at either of them. Atleigh waited on the porch to see Lacey leave.

"What do we do about Mom's ashes?" Atleigh said stiffly. Lacey had her bag in one hand, the car keys in the other.

"You're the one she told about how to handle them," Lacey said. "You should be the one to scatter them."

And she left.

The ride to Durham was quiet. Eight hours of the roar of Eon's car engine and the low mutter of talk radio and the heat of the sun through the windshield. Atleigh spent half of it asleep, leaned up against the door with her head on a balled-up shirt. Her face throbbed from the hit she'd taken the day before, and there was a shiner on her cheek. She didn't wear much makeup, but she made an exception after the looks she got at the first rest stop, dabbing and powdering until the bruise all but disappeared.

She didn't know what to say to Eon. She felt like she ought to apologize. Lacey had called him a parasite, after all, and that probably wasn't sitting well with him. But she was so full of hurt herself, she didn't know how to find the words. So she just stayed in the quiet, huddled around the ache in her chest, which she told herself was because of the fight with Riley, and not the sudden absence of Lacey.

She perked up when Eon got off the highway. That meant they were getting somewhere.

"He goes by Soldier," Eon said.

"Creative."

"Most of them are." Eon quirked his eyebrows. "But his host's name is Sean Larson, and you won't catch him answering to anything else in public. He works in the leech screening office, clearing a path for undetected infiltration."

"So he makes sure some leeches can get into government positions without anybody noticing what they are," she said. "Like the guy running the metal detector at the airport."

"Yeah, basically."

"You ever wonder how we can possibly win this?" Atleigh said, looking out the passenger window at the redbrick buildings they passed. "This is some Hydra shit. Cut off one head and two more grow in its place."

Eon shrugged. "Your thinking is very . . . final. We win, or we lose. We beat them, or we fail." He glanced at her. "Your sister is with you, or she's betrayed you."

"Some things are final," Atleigh said, thinking of the urn in the back seat. "Dead or alive, those are pretty discrete categories."

"All I'm saying is, maybe this isn't one of those situations," Eon said. "Maybe we don't beat them *or* fail. Maybe we just spend our lives chopping the thing's heads off, no matter how many grow back. Maybe the important thing isn't results, but the ongoing fight that started before us and will continue after us."

Atleigh grunted, even though what she really wanted to do was reach across the center console and twist her fingers between his.

"So," she said. *"Sean."*

"Sean," Eon repeated, allowing for the change of subject. "I've got an address. Eight fifty-four Small Pine Boulevard."

Atleigh hesitated.

"Eon," she said. "How did you get an address?"

He looked at her sideways. "I did some things that weren't nice."

"Oh." She frowned at him. "I'm sorry."

"I'm not," he said firmly. "It was Chloe."

Eon parked down the road from the entrance to Hidden Lakes, marked by a wood sign with the name carved into it in cursive. It wasn't hard to spot the guard from across the road, hunched over a small tablet to watch something—it looked like a soap opera, Atleigh decided, as they crept across the road. He was a lacertaform (called "lacies" for short, which had always gotten on Lacey's nerves), so he was gray-green, lizard-like, with an extra pair of arms. Still humanoid, though, so he could sit in a regular chair and look at a screen with a human range of color perception.

Eon and Atleigh bent low, almost in unison, when they drew closer, and moved in short bursts, so close to the little guard station that Atleigh's shoulder scraped the bricks.

She felt like a teenager. Or, really, she felt like what she imagined teenagers felt when they crept out of their parents' houses to greet a handle of vodka in the woods, or to feel their way across each other's bodies in a parking lot somewhere. Atleigh hadn't been that kind of teenager, and mostly, she didn't miss it. It couldn't offer her the same sense of purpose that she felt now, and that was what drove Atleigh when she got tired of the car seat, or the unfamiliar beds, or the thick silver blood that collected under her fingernails.

But Lacey had never had that drive, Atleigh realized. She had come along for the ride, and she had even gotten good at spotting leeches or following leads, but it wasn't where her heart was. Atleigh didn't know where Lacey's heart was. And maybe that was the real problem—not that Lacey wasn't the same as her, but that Atleigh didn't *know* what Lacey really was.

Once they were past the front gate, they found themselves on the side of a straight, neat road lined with houses. There was an island in the middle of the road packed with manicured bushes and flowers. All the houses looked pretty much the same, each of them a muted shade of gray, brown, or white, with a different assemblage of windows and doors, but the same siding, the same central front door, the same two-car garage. There was something nice about the consistency, Atleigh thought, though she wouldn't have admitted it to anyone. This was a place to disappear in.

Atleigh pulled up a map of the place on her phone and walking directions to 854 Small Pine Boulevard. It wasn't a long walk. Atleigh sort of wished it were, so she could get herself together—her breaths were coming fast and shallow, and she couldn't seem to slow them down.

"You know," Eon said, "we don't have to do this."

"Like you said," Atleigh replied. "It was Chloe."

He nodded, and they turned onto Small Pine Boulevard.

When Sean Larson got home from the office, he set down his briefcase, wiped the sweat that had gathered along his hairline, and shrugged off his digital skin. It was only then that he turned on the lights in his kitchen and confronted a young man perched on his island countertop.

"You know," Sean said, "that's marble. I'd rather you not scratch it."

"Scratching is the least of your problems, Sean," the young man replied. "I've had *several* glasses of water here, and I assure you, I did not use a coaster."

"That's rude," Sean pointed out. "And so is coming into a man's house without being invited."

The young man shrugged, and Sean spotted the silver gleaming under his shirt collar.

He did not spot the young woman who had been hiding in the laundry room closet, coming up behind him, her needleknife held aloft and ready to slit his alien form open at the thorax.

Unfortunately for her, however, he heard the squeak of her shoe on the floor, and the slight creak as she applied pressure. He twisted around, throwing an elbow, hitting nothing but throwing her off, so her knife only scraped his shoulder. He ignored the sharp pain, and grabbed the girl's wrist, shoving her up against the refrigerator.

She had short, coppery hair. Fierce brown eyes. Freckles. Familiar.

A weight fell against Sean's shoulders—the boy, coming to the girl's aid. Not that she needed him, because she was already kicking him between the legs, sending a warped, twisted pain through his entire body, so he could barely breathe. The boy pulled Sean's arms behind his back and forced him to his knees, and the girl stood over him, panting, needleknife firmly in hand.

"You killed my mother," she said between breaths.

"I'm sure I did," he said. "And?"

"And I think a person—even a leech—deserves to know why they're being killed," the girl continued. "So now you know."

She was about to strike. He saw the clench in her hand, the resolve in her eyes. And so, with the full strength of the young man bearing down on him, he did the only thing he could think of to delay the inevitable.

"Would you like to know why I killed your mother?" Sean asked, not unkindly.

He could tell by the girl's expression that the answer was yes, even if she didn't know why, even if she had never before paused to ask herself the question.

"She was an obstruction," he said. "I did not target her specifically, or seek to cause you pain. I killed her because she didn't matter to me, as you do not matter to me. Killing me will not sate you because you can't make me care about what I did. You will walk away from this unsatisfied, regardless of what you do."

The girl stared at him for a few seconds, and he wondered if she would put the knife down and burst into tears. She seemed close to it, her eyes brimming with moisture.

She lifted a hand—the one without the knife—and put it on his head, her fingers slipping into his hair. Then they curled, gripping tightly, and she wrenched his head forward. Pain burned through his scalp.

She leaned close and whispered, "I know."

And then everything was gone.

Atleigh washed her hands and weapon in the kitchen sink. Eon called in the death so the government cleanup time would come promptly after their departure. Then they gathered their things and left the house, which was now more like a coffin for Sean Larson, also known as Soldier.

Mom had told her, once, that every death she brought about would be a weight on her shoulders, even if it was righteous, even if it was earned. This was not a burden any person was meant to bear, and yet they bore it.

Her hand brushed Eon's as they walked out of the gated community, and then his caught hers and held on. She welcomed the warmth and the gentle pressure of him. He had known that Sean Larson's death didn't belong to him, without having to ask. He had always known things about her without having to ask.

They walked right past the guard at the entrance, ducking under the bar intended to block cars from driving past without permission. The guard saw them this time, eyes going wide with alarm, and Atleigh waved at him. They crossed the street and walked toward Eon's car, still parked on the grass and gravel that bordered the road.

Only it wasn't alone there.

Parked behind it was a green Volvo.

"What are you doing here?"

Atleigh looked worn, and that was how Lacey knew it was done. The leech who had killed their mother was gone.

"I . . ." Lacey gulped down her nerves. She had always carried stress around in her stomach, prone to vomiting before difficult exams or field tests. It had earned her the nickname "Puker" at school.

Atleigh hadn't let go of Eon's hand. And Eon wasn't flickering, wasn't shifty—his skin was already gone, shrugged off at the first sight of her, like he was daring her to say something to him about it. Eon hadn't said much to her, but she could tell he was fierce by the set of his jaw. That was good, Lacey thought, in some distant part of her brain. Atleigh needed somebody just as fierce as she was.

"I couldn't go back," Lacey blurted out finally. "I mean, literally, I can't. I got expelled. For fighting."

"They expelled you for one fight?" Atleigh said.

"No," Lacey said. "This was sort of a . . . last-straw situation. I actually don't fit in so great there."

Atleigh blinked at her. She was hunched a little, like she was in pain. Even then, she was taller than Lacey, who had always wanted to outgrow her big sister and had never quite managed it. Some things just weren't in the cards.

"I think there's too much of me here. In this." Lacey gestured to the two of them. "And it's like they can all see it, all the time." Her throat tightened. "I thought I didn't like it, but I'd miss it, if it was gone."

Atleigh was still just . . . staring at her. Waiting for her to get to the point, more than likely.

"I'm sorry," she finally said. "If you trust him . . . I do, too. Or I'll try."

"Okay," Atleigh said.

"Okay?" Lacey raised her eyebrows. She had expected to do more groveling than that.

"Yeah," Atleigh said. "Come on. It's at least a three-hour drive to the water."

They bought tickets for a boat ride in Nag's Head, Eon, Atleigh, Lacey, and the urn, which Lacey kept hidden in a sweater. The driver was a nimble arachnoid, standing on four legs and operating the boat with the other four, unaided.

They stood at a railing facing the shore, and when the boat had picked up enough speed, Lacey unwrapped the urn, and Atleigh unscrewed the top. Her hands covered Lacey's, and together they tipped the urn over, so the ashes spilled into the sea.

Atleigh and Eon stood so close their shoulders were pressed together. They traded smiles, and then Atleigh cleared her throat.

"Well, that's done," she said. "On to the next thing."

"What next thing?" Lacey asked.

"Getting you un-expelled," Atleigh said. "Obviously."

"I'm not sure you can do that," Lacey said.

"Sure I can. I'll play up the orphaned-daughter-consumed-by-grief angle," she said. "Mom would support it, I'm pretty sure."

The wind blew Lacey's hair across her face, and she yanked it out of the way.

"I don't want to go back there. I told you, I don't fit in there."

"Then don't fit in," Atleigh said. "Make the place fit around you."

"Atleigh—"

Atleigh grabbed Lacey's hand and looked her dead in the eyes. They were clear and focused.

"Mom told me that when we did this, we were supposed to remember what life is," Atleigh said. "Well, here it is: family. And when someone in your family wants something,

something that's good for them, you want it, too, even if you don't understand it. That ritzy space academy is your future, Lacey. So let's get it back."

Lacey smiled. She wrapped Atleigh up in her arms. Eon was smiling, too, as he looked back to the shore, which was disappearing, flattening to just a dark line on the horizon.

HEARKEN

"Black or red?"

The woman in the lab coat held up two small containers: one with a red substance caked inside it and one with black. It sounded like she was asking Darya a question of taste, rather than the question that defined her future. The only question, Darya believed, that would ever matter this much.

The question was not "Black or red?" It was "Life or death?" And Darya would not have been able to answer before that moment.

She had been seven years old when her father first realized what she could become. Her older sister, Khali, had been playing piano in the living room, an old piece by Schubert. Darya sat on the couch, humming along, a book in her lap.

Her mother dozed in the recliner, her mouth lolling open. Darya thought about drawing a mustache on her face. She wouldn't notice it when she awoke. She would be too dazed by the alcohol. Even at seven, Darya knew. But it was not uncommon, with the world as it was. Half her friends' parents had the same problem.

Darya's father stood in the doorway, listening, a dish towel in his hands. He rubbed it over a plate to the rhythm of the notes, which came in stilted intervals as Khali tried to read the music. Darya stopped humming, irritated. The music was meant to be smooth, and it sounded like Khali was chopping it up into bits.

Khali turned the page and adjusted her hands on the piano as she started a new piece. Darya perked up, letting the book drop into her lap. Her mother snored. Her sister began to play, and Darya stood, walked over to the piano, and stared at her sister's hands. To her the notes sounded *wrong* . . . the intervals were too large, or too small; they did not mesh together in the right way.

"That's wrong," she said, wincing.

"No it's not," said Khali. "How would *you* know?"

"Because I can hear it," she said. "It's supposed to be like *this*."

She reached out and shifted her sister's index finger one note over. Then she moved Khali's pinkie finger, and her middle finger.

"There," said Darya. "Now do it."

Khali rolled her eyes. Darya sighed as the notes came together, ringing as they touched each other.

"Oh," said Khali. Her skin was too dark to reveal a blush, but her sheepish expression betrayed her. "You're right. I read it wrong. It's supposed to be in B minor."

Darya smiled a little, walked back to the couch, and picked up her book again. Her father moved the towel in circles even when it started to squeak against the dry dish.

A few weeks later, Darya's father enrolled her in music classes. There they discovered that Darya had perfect pitch—one of the prerequisites for becoming a Hearkener.

Khali quit piano after Darya surpassed her in skill, which took only a year. It was useless to try to play piano when you were in the same family as a potential Hearkener.

"Come on. Today's the day!"

Darya yawned around her cereal. It was too early to be hungry, but her father had warned her that she would need to eat a good breakfast because today would be a long one. She was going to be tested by the Minnesota School for Hearkeners later that morning to see if she was qualified to enroll, and the test could last several hours. That was a long time for an eight-year-old.

Her mother shuffled into the kitchen in her old robe, which was threadbare at the cuffs. She had a mug of coffee in hand, which Darya eyed suspiciously. Her mother had carried it into the bedroom several minutes ago.

A few weeks before, Darya had found a brown bottle under the sink in her parents' bathroom. She had sniffed it, and its contents burned her nose, and seemed to linger there for several minutes. The bottle and the coffee and her mother's running-together words were part of a familiar pattern that she had always recognized, even before Darya had the language to describe it.

Her mother's eyes wandered across Darya's face.

"Where're you going?" she asked.

"I'm taking Darya to get tested," Darya's father said, too brightly.

"Tested for what?"

"Dar has perfect pitch." Her father set his hand on Darya's head and tousled her hair. "She could be a Hearkener someday."

A Hearkener, to Darya's mother, meant two things: being employed by the government—a stable job; and carrying an expensive piece of equipment, the implant, in your head—which meant immediate evacuation if the country was quarantined. She snorted a little.

"D'you really think you should be getting your hopes up?" Her mother's eyes were cold and critical. Darya couldn't look at them. "Almost nobody becomes a Hearkener."

The little bubble of excitement that had risen inside Darya as soon as she woke up was gone, like it had floated away.

Her father rose and took her mother's arm. "Maybe you should get back to bed, Reggie. You don't look well."

"I just meant," her mother said angrily, "that I don't want her to be *disappointed*—"

"I know," he said.

He ushered her from the room. Darya heard the bedroom door close and muffled voices getting louder every second until something banged shut. No longer hungry, she dumped her cereal bowl into the sink without finishing.

"Your mom's not feeling so good, Dar," her father said as they walked down the sidewalk in front of the apartment building. "She didn't mean it."

Darya nodded without thinking.

They would have lived in the suburbs if they could have—it was safer there, since the attacks came less frequently—but her father's job only paid well enough for a small apartment downtown.

The attacks had always been a part of Darya's life. They could come from anyone, and they were waged against everyone with a pulse. That was why Darya and her sister had to wear face masks on the way to school.

Her father had taught them both to know bio-bombs when they saw them, but their minds had a tendency to wander when they were together, and he didn't trust them to look for bombs yet. Kids at school teased them for the masks, but they couldn't persuade their father to let them go without. "Prove to me that you can pay attention," he always said.

Death was too real a possibility. Most people didn't make it past fifty nowadays, even if they lived in the suburbs.

Her father pulled her tight to his side as they walked, scattering old cans and bits of paper with the toes of their shoes. She craned her neck to see the tops of the buildings—they seemed so far away, though her father said they were shorter than the buildings in most cities. Most of the windows in the building next to her were blown out completely from the days when destructive bombs had been in fashion. But it was the loss of people, not buildings, that made a war destructive, and the fanatics had figured that out.

They stopped walking and stood next to a blue sign marked with graffiti. Darya scratched her leg with her free hand and gazed up at her father. He was not a tall man, nor was he short. His skin was dark brown, like Darya's, and his hair was black and smooth, shiny like her hair, too. He had moved to the States from India before the quarantine. India had been one of the first countries targeted when the attacks began because of its high population. Now the infection was so rampant that the borders had to be closed to prevent a worldwide epidemic. Her father's parents had gotten infected, so they hadn't been able to leave with him. She had never met her grandparents. She assumed they were dead by now.

"Will the test be hard, Daddy?"

He smiled. "Most of it will be things you already know how to do. And the rest you will be able to figure out. Don't worry, Dar. You'll do great."

A bus trundled around the corner as he finished speaking, and creaked to a stop right in front of them. The doors opened, and Darya's father paid the fare. They sat down in the middle, next to an old lady who was shifting her dentures around in her mouth, and across from a middle-aged man with a mask covering his mouth and nose.

Her father leaned in close and whispered, "Okay, so what do we do when we get on a train or a bus?"

"Look for masks," she whispered back. They would have been wearing masks, too, if they had not had to leave the two they owned for Darya's mother, who had to walk Khali to school later, and Khali. Masks were expensive. But she was safe with her father, who could spot a bio-bomb anywhere.

"Why do we do that?"

"Because only people with masks will set off bio-bombs." Her voice dipped even lower at the word *bio-bomb,* as if saying it any louder would provoke an attack.

"Right," he said, "and after we look for masks, what do we do?"

"We watch."

The enemy could be anyone, anywhere. All that they had in common was a commitment to bringing about the apocalypse. They believed the world ought to be destroyed. They did not believe in ending their own lives. Darya didn't understand it and didn't want to try.

He nodded. And they watched, both of them, as the bus bumped and thudded around corners and down streets. Darya had not seen much of the city because she spent all her travel time eyeing the people around her. She was usually in a bus, rather than a train, because buses were easier to escape from.

"You know, when I was young, people didn't like Hearkeners much," her father said.

Darya watched the man across from her. His eyes remained steady on the floor. She could hear his breaths through the slats in the mask—not loud, but louder than unfiltered breaths.

"Why not?" she asked.

"Because they were seen as an unnecessary expenditure," he said. "Not worth the cost, I mean. But the people over at the Bureau for the Promotion of Arts were very insistent that music would help a troubled world. And then when people started dying . . ." He shrugged. "Everyone started to understand why Hearkeners were so important."

"Why are they so important?"

"Because what they hear . . . it's like hearing something beyond us. Something bigger than us." He smiled down at her. "It reminds us that there's more going on in this world than we can see with our eyes and touch with our hands."

Darya didn't quite understand what her father meant, but she knew there was something beautiful in it all the same.

Then she heard something—quickening breaths from the man across from them. She saw a bead of sweat roll down the side of his forehead. He looked so harmless—he was short, with salt-and-pepper hair and a white collared shirt. His slacks were pressed, creased. He was not a killer. But the peculiar blend of fear and determination in his eyes was enough to make Darya hold her breath.

As the man in the mask moved to get off the bus, he took a canister from his bag and dropped it on the ground. It was an object she had only seen in pictures—dull metal, about six inches long, as thick as her wrist, with an opening at one end to let out the gas.

Someone screamed. Darya's father clapped his hand over her mouth and nose, and lifted her up from the abdomen. He ran toward the front of the bus, shoving people out of his way with his elbows. Darya fought for air, but the hand prevented her from taking a breath.

Her father shouldered his way out the bus door. Against her will, Darya's body began to struggle against her father's grasp, fighting for air. Her father sprinted down the street and into an alley just as she began to see spots.

He took his hand from her mouth, and she gasped.

He had not had time to cover his own mouth. What if he inhaled some of the gas? What if he was infected? She choked on a sob. What if he died?

"It's okay, Dar." He gathered her close to his chest. "I held my breath. We're all right. We're just fine."

Technically, the only distinguishing feature of a Hearkener was the implant. It was placed in the temporal lobe of the brain. It didn't protrude from the skin, but it contained a dye that created a weblike pattern on the right temple. Hearkeners were required to pull their hair away from their faces to reveal the pattern. Its purpose was to make them easily identifiable.

The implant made them what they were. They heard music everywhere—as long as there were people, there was music.

The first time she saw a licensed Hearkener was outside the Minnesota School for Hearkeners, on the fifth step from the bottom of thirty long, low steps. They had not made it to the testing center the day of the bio-bomb, but they went three days later, this time walking the whole way instead of taking the bus.

Her father stood beside her, clutching her hand. They both paused to watch the Hearkener woman walk past.

She was tall and slender, with hair the color of earth and the same pale skin Darya's mother had. She walked without a bounce in her step, but at the same time, her feet were light on the cement. She wore a knee-length coat that snapped when the wind caught it. The pattern on her temple was iodine-black, but it was the last thing Darya noticed.

All Darya could think was that this Hearkener of Death was the most beautiful woman she had ever seen, and she wanted to be just like her.

As the Hearkener passed Darya and her father, she tilted her head, the way a person does when they are trying to hear something. Her footsteps slowed for just a moment, and she closed her eyes.

After the moment passed, she looked Darya's father in the eye and smiled. Despite the curl of her lips, a troubled look remained in her eyes. She kept walking.

Three weeks later, Darya's father died of the infection, and that Hearkener was the only person who ever heard his death song.

Darya passed the test, and her mother enrolled her in the Minnesota School for Hearkeners that fall. Though Darya's mind was still muddled with grief, it was what her father had wanted for her, so she went.

Her first impression of the place was that it was too large for her. Even the front steps were vast, made of wide slabs of a dark, matte stone. The building itself was tall, made of black glass with girders that formed a huge X across the front. A giant clock, fixed to the front of the building, told her she had five minutes to get to her first class.

She looked at the piece of paper the school had sent her, along with half a dozen packets and information sheets, to tell her where to go on her first day. All the new students took classes together until they tested into particular levels of musical study or until they chose their instrument specialties.

The schedule said: *Hour 1, Introduction to Hearkener Study, Room A104.*

Darya looked up when she passed through the doors. She couldn't see much past the security barrier. A stern-looking man in a black uniform told her to put her bag on a black conveyor belt that would take it through a scanner. She then had to stand in what looked like a globe with a tunnel cut through it so that it could scan her body. She had gone through both when she took her tests here, but her father had been with her then. This time she was afraid. What if they didn't let her through?

But another man, on the other side, handed her the bag and let her pass him. The hallway here was completely different from the dingy, green-tiled hall that had been in her old school. Here, the floors were white marble—or at least something that looked like marble—and the walls were navy blue.

Even the lockers were elegant—made of dark wood, they lined the walls as far as she could see.

She looked at the first room she passed—Room A101. She was close. She walked past another section of lockers, and glanced at the rooms to her left and right. A104 was on the left. Taking a deep breath, she walked in.

The room was oddly silent. Ten other children her age sat at long wooden tables inside. She found an empty seat near the back, next to a densely freckled boy tapping out a rhythm on the table with his pencil.

The bell rang. An older woman with gray curly hair and a chunk missing from her eyebrow strode in. She wore the Hearkener uniform: a black trench coat, buttoned up to her throat, and gray pants. Darya leaned to the side to see what color the woman's implant was. Red. That meant she heard life songs rather than death songs.

The woman cleared her throat, though there was no reason to—no one was talking.

"Hello," she said. "Let's not bother with introductions. Oh, except me. We go by surnames here, and mine is Hornby. I'll be giving you the rundown of Hearkener history."

Darya knew the basics—that the Hearkener implant had something to do with string theory, and what it did was channel the vibrations of the human body somehow and make them into music. But she felt strangely exposed, without knowing more.

"String theory became widely accepted in the early part of the century," Hornby said. "Can anyone tell me what string theory is, basically? Yes—how about you—what's your name?"

The boy next to Darya had raised his hand. "Christopher Marshall, ma'am."

"'Hornby' will do, Marshall. Go ahead."

"String theory is the theory that subatomic particles are one-dimensional strings instead of three-dimensional, and that the one-dimensional strings form the fabric of the universe."

"Good," said Hornby. "Also, the strings are constantly vibrating. That's important to remember because when Dr. Rogers created the first implant, all it did was channel the vibrations and their various frequencies and translate them into music. It was her successor, Dr. Johnson, who refined the implant to filter out all frequencies but those of human cells, so it was only people who made music. Anyone want to tell me why he would do a thing like that? You there—your name . . . ?"

"Samanth—uh, I mean Brock," a girl in the front row said.

"He said he just wanted to see if it was possible."

"In fact, that is what he said, but we have since determined it was so he could hear the music his dying wife made." Hornby added, "He had a friend try out the implant so that she could transcribe the music. She was the first Hearkener. But the implants didn't stop there."

Here she paused and tapped the red dye on her temple with her index finger.

"The last developer of the implant discovered that he could filter out either the vibrations of decaying cells or the vibrations of regenerating cells. In other words, he could make the implant play the sound of a person's life or the sound of their death. For a long time, hardly any Hearkeners chose to hear death songs. Now that death is so common, those Hearkeners are in high demand."

Darya remembered the look the Hearkener who had heard her father's death song had given him. She had seemed almost bewitched by it. Darya didn't think that woman had chosen the death songs because they were in higher demand.

Hornby clapped her hands. "Now that that's out of the way, I would like to call each of you up so that I can listen to your life song and tell you what instruments it seems to include. I say 'seems' because there are obviously no actual instruments involved in a person's life song. Certain sounds merely remind us of certain instruments. This is important because, in your first year here, you will be selecting two of the three instruments you are required to master. Much of your time will be spent trying out each of them to see which ones you gravitate toward. Hopefully my evaluation will steer you in the right direction."

It had been a very brief history lesson. Darya sat in her seat with her hands clutched around the edge of the chair as each of the eleven children in the class walked up to the front of the room so Hornby could listen to them. She didn't want to go. She didn't want to let that woman analyze her. She didn't know why, but it felt far too personal, far too intimate for a setting like this.

It wasn't long before Hornby pointed to her and bent her finger, beckoning Darya forward. Darya got up—too fast; she knocked the chair over and had to set it right again—and walked to the front of the room, her hands fidgeting at her sides. When she stood in front of Hornby, the woman asked her, "Your name?"

"Darya Singh," she said.

"Singh." Hornby laughed a little. "Well, that's convenient.

Let me listen to you for a bit."

Hornby focused her attention on Darya's face, though she wasn't exactly looking into Darya's eyes. She stared for a few seconds, and then a few more seconds . . . and then Darya became aware that Hornby had been staring at her for much longer than she had stared at anyone else . . . and then Hornby rocked on her heels, as if something had blown her backward.

"My goodness," she said quietly. Then she seemed to come to her senses, and said, more briskly, "I hear . . . violin, cello, piano, some voice, trombone, trumpet, drum . . . there are more, but those are the dominant instruments."

She leaned a little closer to Darya's face, so that Darya could see a dart of blue in her otherwise green eyes.

"I've never heard so much dissonance in a life song before," she said quietly, so that only Darya could hear.

And that was the beginning of Darya's education as a Hearkener.

"When do you get the implant?"

Darya stabbed a piece of lettuce with her fork. After seven years at Hearkener school, she had passed the final test, an achievement half of her class hadn't managed. And all Khali wanted to know was when she would get to work. But that was Khali—all work and no play.

"A week from tomorrow," she said.

"Oh."

"It's soon, I know."

Khali frowned. "What?"

"A week. It's hardly enough time to determine my entire future."

Khali's expression was still blank. Darya felt like she had started speaking another language without meaning to. She raised her eyebrows at her older sister.

It was midday, but the windows were boarded up, so it felt like night in the kitchen. Wood wouldn't keep the infection at bay if someone set off a bio-bomb nearby, but it was better than nothing. The battery-operated lantern on the table glowed orange, with fake flickers so that it imitated fire.

Khali lived with their mother now, in their childhood home. Darya had stopped coming back during the holidays three years before, and now only saw Khali when they went out to eat, or when she was sure her mother would be asleep.

"I don't understand," Khali said. "What decision needs to be made?"

"*The* decision." Darya scowled. "You know—life songs or death songs? It's a huge choice. It changes everything."

"But you're going to choose death songs," Khali replied tersely. "Right? Because you want to record Mom's song before it's too late. Right?"

Darya pushed the piece of lettuce around her plate.

"She's only got a few weeks left if she doesn't get the transplant. At most, Darya."

Darya did know.

"She won't get another Hearkener! We don't have enough money as it is!" Khali was shaking her head. "I can't believe you wouldn't do this for her. I can't believe you."

Darya looked up, her lips pursed.

"I can't believe *you*," she said. "She's already controlled my life enough; I'm not going to let her control the rest of it, too!"

"What do you mean? She hasn't controlled you."

"What little childhood we had she took from us," said Darya. "Kids aren't supposed to think, 'Oh, Mommy's drunk again, so I'd better stay away from her.' Kids aren't supposed to take care of their parents. We've done enough for her. I'm not doing *this* for her."

Khali's mouth was open, but she wasn't saying anything. She just looked stunned.

Then she said, "You've only met the real her a few times, Darya. The woman you know is just the alcohol, stifling her."

"The implant isn't something you can undo, Khali. You choose death, you choose it forever. You can't tell me it's my duty to choose something just because our shitty mom is finally getting what was always coming to her."

Darya clutched the edge of the table, waiting for Khali to scream at her, or call her names, or something. But Khali's eyes just filled with tears, and her lower lip started to wobble.

"Then . . ." She gulped. "Don't do it for her. Do it for me, so I can hear. . . . She's the only parent I . . . Please, Darya."

Darya carried her plate to the sink and scraped the remnants of her salad into the garbage disposal. She took a long time to clean her plate, scraping slowly, rinsing slowly. She didn't want Khali to see the tears in her own eyes.

"I don't know if I can," she finally said.

"Black or red?" the nurse asked again.

All her life Darya had been developing a resistance to obligation of any kind. No one had taught her to; maybe the world had taught her to. People who set off bio-bombs did so out of a religious obligation to hasten the apocalypse. The pictures she had seen of the bombers did not reveal any delight in the prospect of the world ending—they tried to stay alive in the aftermath of their attacks only so that they could attack again.

Obligation was dangerous because it muddled the mind. Did she want to choose red to defy her mother or because she really wanted it? Did she want to choose black for her sister's sake? How could she know what she really wanted with so many competing obligations—to herself, to her mother, to her sister, to her late father?

Darya remembered the Hearkener's face as she listened to Darya's father's death song, distress and warmth competing for dominance, like she protected a secret, and Darya longed to understand it. It was that whisper of longing that made the decision for her.

"Black," she said.

The nurse put the red cylinder aside and set the black cylinder on a tray next to the hospital bed. She wrapped rubber tubing around Darya's arm to make the veins stand out. Darya felt her pulse in each one of her fingertips, and a harsh sting as the needle went in. The nurse removed the rubber tubing and, with a small smile, flipped the switch that would start the IV drip.

Darya was supposed to be awake for the procedure, so the

doctors would know they hadn't damaged her brain while inserting the implant. But she wouldn't remember any of it, thanks to whatever was in the IV bag, and she was grateful. She didn't want to remember them peeling back her scalp and drilling into her skull and inserting things into her temporal lobe, the part of the brain that processed sound.

A haze of images was all she retained to remind her that time had passed. Gradually she became aware of someone sitting in front of her, but it looked like she was hidden behind a white film. Then a face surfaced, and it was Khali's. Her mouth was moving, but Darya couldn't hear her. There was something over her ears.

Khali covered her eyes momentarily, as if chastising herself, and then took out a pad of paper and a pen. On it, she wrote, *They don't want you to hear anyone yet. Said it would be too overwhelming. Keep the ear covers on. How do you feel?*

Darya's head throbbed, especially over the right side, where the implant was. Other than that, she just felt heavy, like she could drop right through the mattress.

She didn't want to try to explain all that to Khali, so she just put her thumb up and tried to smile, though she was sure it looked more like a grimace. Even her cheeks were heavy.

Khali's eyes were wet. She scribbled another note on the pad:

Thank you.

Darya knew what Khali was thanking her for. If she hadn't been so tired, she might have tried to say that she had not made her choice for Khali, had not made it for their mother—that she wasn't even sure she wanted to hear her mother's song, despite what she had chosen. But soon the weight collected behind her eyes, dragging her back to sleep.

She woke up later to dark skies showing between the blinds, and a nurse peering at the incision in her scalp. They had buzzed some of her hair—eight square inches of it, in fact. She had demanded to know the exact amount.

Darya's mother had had beautiful hair when she was younger, a reddish brown that shone like a penny in sunlight. It had come down to the middle of her back, incorrigibly wavy—no matter how hard she tried to straighten it, it refused to stay that way. Darya had often thought it was a shame her mother's hair would die with her, even though she liked her own the way it was.

It was a strange thing, but in the moments right before she fully woke, a memory of her mother had come to mind, from one of her sober streaks. Darya had come home from school for spring break, and her mother had been restored—one month sober, rosy-cheeked, smart, pleasant. She and Khali had been making cake batter in the kitchen as Darya's neighbor nailed boards on all the windows, and her mother had been singing in a thin soprano.

"Sing with me!" her mother had said. "You have a beautiful voice, Darya."

She had started on a song that Darya knew, and though Darya had felt that this woman was a stranger, she could not help but join in. She had made up a harmony on the spot, slipping her lower voice beneath her mother's, and tears—happy ones—had come into her mother's eyes.

"Beautiful," she had said.

That was the week Darya chose violin as her third instrument, even though her fingertips were too soft for the strings, and she had trouble holding her fingers in tension for so long. She chose it not because she liked it, but because it was challenging, because she knew bearing through the pain would result in greater joy.

The nurse checking the incision site noticed that Darya was awake, and she smiled. She said something Darya couldn't hear, thanks to the glorified earmuffs she still wore. The nurse removed her rubber gloves and tossed them into a nearby trash can. Darya was finally awake enough to look around—she was in a large room full of beds, with curtains separating each one. She could only see the toes of the patient next to her.

A stack of books stood on the bedside table—some of Khali's favorites and some of her own. Darya slid one of Khali's from the stack and started to read, propping herself up on the pillows.

About an hour later, Khali walked into the room, dabbing at one of her eyes with a handkerchief. Her face was discolored—she had obviously been crying. *My face looks like raw hamburger when I cry,* Khali used to say. *It's so embarrassing. I can never hide it.*

Khali clutched a phone in her right hand, the one without the handkerchief. Her grip was so tight it looked like she was about to crack the battery in half with her fingernails.

"What?" Darya said. She could feel the word vibrating in her throat, but she had no idea how loudly she had spoken. Khali didn't shush her, so she assumed it hadn't been that loud.

Khali picked up the notebook and pencil resting next to the stack of books, and started to write.

Mom's request for a liver transplant was denied.

Darya nodded. Obviously. They didn't give new livers to alcoholics.

I had her transferred here, so she'll be close to us. She's in room 3128.

Darya wanted her mother to be as far away as possible.

She looks awful.

Khali glanced at her, wide-eyed, waiting. *Waiting for what?* Darya wondered, but it was a silly question. She knew what Khali was waiting for: an offer. *I'll go record her death song for you.*

But Darya didn't offer. She took the pad of paper from her sister's hands and scribbled, *Okay. Thanks for telling me.*

It was midnight. Khali had left hours ago, right after Darya wrote back to her, but not in a huff—that was not Khali's way. She always made sure to smile when she said good-bye.

Darya put her feet over one side of the bed and let them dangle for a moment before touching them to the tile. It was cold, or her feet were warm from being buried under blankets for so long. She stretched her arms up and felt her back crack and pop, though she didn't hear it. The ear covers were still on her head.

She walked into the bathroom and looked at her reflection. What she saw shocked her. She had not expected the implant to transform her the way it had. The black veins sprawled across her temple, arching over her eyebrow and down to her cheekbone. She turned her head to see how far back the dye had traveled—it stretched over her scalp as far as the bandage that covered the incision site. Soon her hair would grow over it.

She touched the layer of fuzz that was already growing in. It would grow back faster than normal hair, she knew—the nurse had told her, with a wink, that she had put some hair-regrowing salve on it, the kind they used for vain men and cancer patients. Looking at her reflection, Darya didn't think she would have minded keeping the shaved portion for a while. It made her look tough, just like the implant dye.

She made sure the back of her gown was tied tightly, slipped her shoes on, and walked down the hallway. At the end of it was a large waiting room that looked out over the city. The hospital was one of the taller buildings in this part of Minneapolis, so she would be able to see more than usual.

She shuffled down the hallway, her head aching, but not enough to stop her. In one corner of the waiting room, by the television screen, were what looked like a brother and sister. The sister was rocking back and forth, her hands pressed between her knees. Both stared at the television, but were not really staring at the television.

Standing near the window on the other end of the room was a young man with the same ear covers she wore, but his whole head was buzzed instead of just eight inches of it. When

he looked to the side, she recognized him as Christopher Marshall.

He smiled at her and beckoned for her to come closer. She did, scanning the tables for something she could write on. But then she saw that he was already holding a notebook, balancing it against the railing near the windows, and there was a pen behind his ear.

She stood next to him and touched her fingertips to his chin, to turn his head. She wanted to see which implant he had chosen. The red dye sprawled across his forehead disappointed her. She had hoped that their paths would intersect in the future, but if he had chosen life songs, he would be in different classes for the next two years, and work in different places thereafter.

He wrote something on the pad of paper:

What made you choose it?

She sighed, and took the pen from him. She paused with the tip of the pen over the paper for a few seconds before she began to write, then scribbled out what she had written and began again. It took her several tries to find a response she liked: *Life's something we already understand. Death is a mystery.*

He nodded, looking impressed, and wrote, *I've heard dying people are ornery toward Hearkeners. Hornby got that scar above her eyebrow because one of her clients chucked an alarm clock at her head.*

Darya laughed, and reached across him to write back. *So is that why you picked life? You can just wear a helmet, you know.*

He shook his head. *No.* ~~*I guess I just wanted to*~~ *People don't celebrate life as much as they used to. I think they should.*

She nodded and leaned her elbows on the railing. He did the same thing next to her. Their arms, side by side, were as different as the paths they had chosen—his were long and pale, dotted with freckles, hers were brown and short.

The city lights were beautiful at night, glowing from distant offices and blinking atop buildings, like the Christmas lights her father had put up because he liked the way they looked, though he only turned them on for an hour a day to save on the electric bill. But there was no limit on these lights—they would be on all night, as long as it was dark enough to see them.

Christopher was writing in the notebook again.

Have you listened to anyone yet?

She shook her head.

He bit his lip and wrote, *Do you mind if I listen to you?*

Darya hesitated. Hearkeners had listened to her life song before, but this was different. This was his first one, and he wanted it to be her? She doubted he was thinking of it that way, but it seemed that way to her.

You can say no. I just want it to be someone I know, not whoever runs into me first when I walk out of the hospital, he wrote.

He made a good point. She would be the first, but she would also be the first of many. She took the pen from him and said, *Go ahead.*

He took off his ear covers, slowly, so they didn't slip and hit the incision site. She turned to face him, though she knew it wouldn't be any easier for him to hear her song if he was looking at her. He stood with the ear covers clutched in front of him for a few seconds, frowning and squinting as he made sense of the new sounds in his mind.

Then, after a few seconds, he stopped squinting or frowning. His face relaxed, and his mouth drifted open, forming a loose O. Darya shifted, holding the railing with one hand, uncomfortable as he stared at her. And he *stared.* His eyes, normally so courteous, were wide and *on* her, pressing against her until she was forced to look back at him.

When she did, she saw a tear in his eyelashes. He wiped it with the back of his hand and shoved the ear covers back on.

Did he not want to hear her anymore? Had it hurt him?

Far from staring now, he was looking at his shoes, at the railing, at anything but her. After she had let him listen to her, after she had exposed that part of herself to him, he had nothing to say, not even a glance to give?

She handed him the notebook, and the pen, and walked away without another written word.

Darya walked the hallways of the hospital for a long time after that, not sure where she was half the time. She walked through a cafeteria, and an atrium full of plants in large clay pots, and a hectic corridor with gurneys lining the walls. At 2:00 a.m., she realized that she was in a hallway in which all the rooms started with a 31. Sighing, she walked until she found room 3128 and peered through the window next to the door.

Her mother, with her now-scraggly red hair and yellow-tinged skin, lay in the bed, hooked up to an IV and a few monitors. Khali sat beside her mother with her head on the edge of the mattress, fast asleep. Resting against the wall was a violin case. There in case Darya changed her mind, probably.

Not for the first time, Darya wondered what it was that made Khali so attached to their mother. Their father had told her once that their mother hadn't started drinking until two years after Darya was born, when Khali was seven. There wasn't an inciting incident as far as Khali knew—no great losses, or deaths, or arguments—but the strain of the world had weighed on their mother always, more than it weighed on other people. And she had cracked under that weight.

A sad story, maybe, but Darya did not feel particularly sympathetic. The world was terrible for everyone these days, and they still got up, got dressed, went to work, kept their families together.

It didn't really matter, though, did it? It didn't matter whether she felt sympathy or not. Khali had asked her for something. Khali had always been there for her. And Darya would give it to her.

She opened the door. The sound roused Khali from sleep, but not their mother. Khali stared at her sister like she was an apparition, and Darya supposed she did look like one, in a pale hospital gown, her hair half shaved, wandering in uncertainly. The door closed behind her.

She walked to the violin case, and crouched over it to open it. Khali had probably brought the violin because it was so portable; she could not have known how perfect it was for this occasion. Darya had chosen it as her third instrument because it was so difficult for her. It seemed only fitting that she should play it on an occasion that would also be difficult for her.

Usually Hearkeners listened to death songs with a computer in hand instead of an instrument, to transcribe the music so that it could be preserved and played later. Khali didn't have a computer to bring, and neither did Darya, so the instrument would have to do.

She sat down in a chair opposite Khali, with their mother between them. Khali opened her mouth to speak, her eyes full of tears, and Darya pressed her finger to her lips. She didn't want to hear Khali's gratitude—it might make her too stubborn, might make her want to take back what she had already done.

Darya reached up and removed her ear covers. She put them on the floor and set her violin in her lap. She understood, then, why Christopher's face had screwed up when he took his ear covers off. At first all she heard were sounds—clapping and clamping and stomping and banging. She scowled for a few seconds as the sounds transformed into notes . . . into instruments.

And then the song of her mother's dying came to life in her mind.

The notes were low and consistent, at first, like a cello solo—but not like a solo, more like a bass line. And then, arching above it was something high and sweet—painfully sweet—faster than the cellos—but not too fast, not frantic. Then the low notes and the high notes melded together into one melody, twisting around each other, straightening out in harmonies. She thought of the song she and her mother had sung in the kitchen. Her mother had had cake batter on her fingers.

Darya stared at her mother the way Christopher had stared at her, *staring*, trying to extract from her mother's face the genius of this song. It took a few seconds before she realized her mother was awake—awake and staring back.

The melody changed, turning darker. If it had had a flavor, it would have been unsweetened chocolate, bitter, smooth. Her mother's eyes were on hers, clearer than they had been for the years that Darya lived with her, but bloodshot, ugly. She remembered the night she had awoken to her mother breaking plates in the kitchen, raging at their father for one reason or another. She felt a surge of anger.

But still the music went on, lifting again, swelling, louder. It was so loud Darya moved to plug her ears, but she couldn't plug her ears against this song, she couldn't block out the sound of her mother's death. The sound of her ending.

Loud and pounding, a heartbeat contained in a song, low and high, vibrating in Darya's head. Even if there had been a thousand symphonies playing alongside it, Darya still would have picked it out from the rest—it was insistent—she had to hear it—she picked up the violin and wedged it between her chin and her shoulder.

Darya didn't know what to play first. There were too many competing melodies at work in this complex death song, hard to pick just one. Finally she isolated what seemed to be the

dominant notes and began to play them. She had not been in school long enough to be good at this, but she remembered what she had learned: Listen first, and trust your fingers to play what you've just heard. Don't listen to yourself; listen to the song.

Darya trusted her fingers. She played furiously, her eyes squeezed shut and her jaw clenched, as the song swelled again, the notes turning over and over each other. Her arms ached and her head throbbed but still she played, not for her mother and not for herself and not for Khali anymore, but because the song required her to play, to find its strongest moments and bring them to the surface so that someone else could hear them.

Her fingers slowed, then, finding the melody she had heard first, the low, persistent notes. They moved into the high, sweet notes, the notes that hit each other so hard she thought they might crack each other in half. They were weak like her mother was weak, sprawled on the couch in her nightgown—but beautiful like her mother, too. They were the smiles that surfaced in the afternoon, when her mother was more lucid, and the happy tears she cried over her daughter's voice, and the light fingers that went through Darya's hair as she brushed it on her better mornings.

And then the notes were low again, low and slow and barely changing, barely moving, a vague utterance in near solitude. They were the weight, the weight her mother bore, the world that defeated her.

The song, moving in Darya's brain—melodic—dissonant—fast—slow—low—beautiful . . .

Then she felt tears on her face, and she threw the violin onto the bed and ran.

She ran. She heard pieces of songs all around her and clapped her hands over her ears, but it did her no good. The world was *loud*, too loud to bear. Still, no matter how far she ran, she could hear her mother's death song in her memory, the most powerful of all the music she encountered in her sprint back to the room.

The nurse saw her on her way back in and grabbed her by the arm. "Where are your ear covers? Where have you been?"

Darya just shook her head. The nurse ran down the hall and returned a few seconds later, new ear covers in her hands. She shoved them over Darya's ears, and all the music stopped. Relief flooded Darya's body like cold water. The nurse steered her away.

Darya crawled onto her bed, gathered her knees to her chest, and stared at the opposite wall.

She slept past noon. Khali came in to speak to her, even touched her hand lightly, but she pretended she couldn't feel it. She had done what her sister wanted, but she had not done it with a good heart; she had done it out of obligation, something she had always avoided. And she felt angry—angry with herself, for doing it, and angry with Khali, for making her feel like she had to, and angry at the death song itself, for refusing to leave her alone from the second she awoke.

Darya sat in bed for the rest of the day, eating small spoonfuls of flavored gelatin and watching the news report on an attack that had happened in Kansas City that morning. She stared at the death tolls, numb. Sometimes it was weeks before a person showed signs of infection, and sometimes it was minutes—it depended on the potency of the bio-bomb. How long would it be before the world ran out of people?

Darya winced as part of her mother's death song played in her mind again. It ached inside her, feeble but intricate, and every few seconds she felt tears pinching behind her eyes like tweezers. She tried to suppress them, but they came anyway, blurring the news. She didn't know what to do, so she just sat there.

That evening she left her food uneaten on her tray and walked down the hallway again to the waiting room. There were more people in it now, most of them reading magazines or staring at the clock. And Christopher was there, too, sitting in one of the chairs with a stack of paper in his lap. His eyes moved straight to her when she walked in.

He beckoned to her again. His ear covers were off now, and he looked slightly agitated, twitching at sounds she couldn't hear. But the songs didn't seem to pain him. Maybe he had learned to tune them out.

She sat down next to him, and removed her own ear covers. This time she didn't hear a series of random sounds when they were off—she heard music right away, everywhere, but not as loud here as it had been in the rest of the hospital. These people weren't sick.

Everyone had a death song, no matter how young or healthy they were, and everyone had a life song, even when they were dying. Everyone was both dying and living at the same time, but the death song grew louder as death approached, just as the life song was loudest at a person's birth. She could hear Christopher's death song, so faint it was barely over a whisper, but she thought she could hear an organ in it, and a clear voice.

"I stayed here all day, hoping you would come back," he said. "I wanted to tell you I was sorry for last night, how I acted."

"You could have asked them for my room number," she said.

He frowned, like this hadn't occurred to him.

"Well," he said, "it felt more like paying penance, this way."

Darya couldn't help it—she smiled a little. Then she remembered how hastily he had shoved the ear covers back on, and her smile faded.

"It was overwhelming," he said. "Your song. I couldn't get it out of my mind. Even while I was listening, it was too much . . . it was too much to bear, so I had to stop." He showed her the first sheet on the stack of paper he was holding. Written at the top was *Daria*. She ignored the misspelling and stared at what was beneath it—crudely rendered musical notes, line after line of them.

"I wrote some of it down," he said. "Do you want to hear it?"

Did she want to hear her life song? Of course she did.

Slowly, Darya nodded.

"Come on, then," he said. He reached for her hand, and led her out of the waiting room. Darya stared at their joined hands as they walked through the hospital corridors. Then she stared at the side of his face, which was also covered in freckles, but these weren't as dark as the ones on his arms, except on his long, narrow nose.

He led her to a set of double doors. The one on the left was marked *Chapel.* Christopher pushed it open, and they walked down the aisle between the pews. No one was inside, which was good, because he was heading straight for the piano.

He sat down on the bench and put the first few sheets of music on the stand. He looked at her furtively from beneath his eyebrows, set his hands on the keys, and began to play.

At first the song was unfamiliar—a few chords, some isolated notes, slow and methodical. After a few seconds she felt like she recognized it from somewhere, though she could not have said where. Was it simply that a person always recognized their own life song, whether they had heard it or not? Because it belonged to them, maybe?

His fingers moved faster, pressing harder into the keys. The notes swelled, became *loud,* fierce, as if giving a voice to her own anger. And then, when they began to clash, she knew where she recognized them from.

She put her hands on the piano, an octave above Christopher's, and played, as best she could, the section of her mother's death song that had been going through her mind since the night before. It fit in perfectly with a section of her life song. It was not quite harmony but not quite repetition—sections of notes matched up perfectly, and other sections layered above her life song, bringing out by contrast its richness, and still other sections were similar but came just a second too late, like her mother's song was chasing her own across the piano.

And she realized that her mother was like her—angry, weak, complex, sensitive—everything, good and bad, moving together in this song that made Darya's song more beautiful. Darya had never seen the similarities before, but they were there—buried, but emerging in her mother's occasional lucidity, emerging in Khali's memories of a woman Darya had barely known, and now, emerging in Darya herself.

She felt herself smile, and then laugh, and then cry, and then all at once.

"It's not exactly beautiful," Christopher said as he played the last note on the last page. He glanced at her. "I don't mean that as an insult. I'm very attached to it. It keeps following me around."

When she didn't respond, he looked slightly alarmed. "I'm sorry, was that rude?"

Darya shook her head, and set her left hand on top of his right, guiding it to the right keys. His fingers warmed hers. He glanced at her, smiling a little.

"Play that again," she said quietly, pointing at the place in the music where the section began. She took her hands from the piano, and listened as Christopher played the section again.

She closed her eyes and swayed without knowing it to the rhythm of the notes.

She had been wrong to say that death was the mystery, not life.

VIM AND

VIGOR

Edie bent over her tablet, stylus in hand, reviewing her sketch. Vigor, the super-strong heroine of the Protectors, stood on the edge of a building, her fingertips bloodied from clawing a stone in half. Edie had dotted Vigor's nose and furrowed brow with freckles as an homage to the fan-fiction writer whose work she was adapting into fan art.

It was almost done. She just had to get Vigor's cape to look like it was fluttering.

After the day she'd had, she was glad to have a distraction. She had been asked to prom—twice. And though her friend Arianna insisted it was a "nonblem"— a problem that wasn't really a problem, like having too much money to fit in your wallet—Edie still felt short of breath. And not in a good way.

She shaded the underside of the cape, the corner tipping up in the wind. Vigor was one of four superheroines in "the Protectors," a line of comics featuring Edie's favorite superheroines. Vigor was half of a duo with her sister, Vim. They developed superpowers after being exposed to a radioactive explosion. Separately, Vim had boundless energy, never requiring sleep, and Vigor had super strength, but together they could summon a crackling, destructive energy they called the Charge.

Her phone buzzed against the desk. She leaned over to

read the new message. Arianna, of course.

Arianna: Pros for going to prom with Evan: good-looking, smart, good conversationalist. Cons: Pretentious. Totally corrected my grammar that one time.

Edie scowled at her phone. Arianna was just trying to be helpful, but she had been hounding Edie about her decision all day. She had a point about Evan, though. Their flirtatious friendship formed around smoke breaks in the field across from the high school during their lunch hour. He was the only person who would talk to her about the human brain for more than five minutes. But all the stories he read were about listless men who didn't care about anything or anyone, and he had asked her to prom between two puffs of a cigarette.

Edie: Well you did use "between" instead of "among."

Arianna: Shush.

Arianna: Pros for Chris: hot, funny, allegedly a good kisser. Cons: You dated him for a year, so high potential for drama.

She had loved Chris Williams once. Or at least, that was how it had seemed, in the dark in the back of his car with his hands on her, or swimming in the lake behind his house in the heat of summer. She loved the glow of his smile against his dark skin, and the way he always opened doors for people, even if it made him late. But their relationship had been like a house with no foundation—one little storm washed it away.

Well, maybe it was more than a little storm.

It had been a heap of twisted metal and a wooden box lowered into the earth.

Edie's stylus wobbled on the tablet screen, and she swore, hurriedly erasing the stray line that ruined Vigor's cape. She had that hot, tight feeling in her throat again. She'd gotten another text, and it sat open on her desk, waiting for a response.

555-263-9888: Hey! It's Lynn. Want to go with us to see the Vim and Vigor movie tonight?

Lynn had attached a selfie, and in it she was wearing Transforma's signature purple lipstick, her lips pouted in an air kiss.

Lynn was one half of what was left of the Protectors Comics Club Edie joined in middle school. Originally, there were four members—Edie, Kate (the founder), Lynn, and Amy—just as there were four superheroines in the Protectors—Vim, Vigor, Transforma, and Haze—so they had each taken on a superheroine name and identity. It was cool at the time.

They had been all but inseparable for four years. Then Kate, who was always full of questionable ideas, suggested they drive to the local 7-Eleven for slushees one night, even though she only had a learner's permit. It was supposed to be a twenty-minute quest for sugar, and it ended in a car crash.

Amy was gone now, her resting place marked by a simple headstone in the Serene Hills Cemetery just outside of town, with a little slot for her data next to her name. At such a young age, her "data" amounted to a few files of childhood artwork and her school records.

555-263-9888: Opening weekend! (!!!!111!)

At one time, the Protectors Comics Club had talked *incessantly* about a movie based on Vim and Vigor coming out, but it had looked unlikely until last year. Kate even texted Edie when the movie's release date was announced, but Edie hadn't known what to say back to her. And now it was here, and she didn't know what to do—not about prom, not about Kate and Lynn, not about anything.

Deep breaths, she told herself. Her therapist told her not to fight the anxiety when it happened, to just count her breaths and accept it. She tried that. When her heart was still racing a few minutes later, she fished around in her purse for the little tin of pills that had been prescribed for exactly this purpose. Her fingers felt clumsy, almost numb. Edie popped one of the pills in her mouth and swallowed it dry.

Then she typed a reply to Lynn.

Sure. Time and place? Gotta support the cause.

They always talked about the Protectors like that, as more than just a bunch of comics. They were a cause, because they were stories about women being heroes, not just spunky reporters or love interests who were sacrificed to the latest villain.

After the text sent, she picked up her stylus and started to draw again.

Edie waited outside the theater for Lynn and Kate, her little purse clutched close, feeling self-conscious. She spotted Kate from a distance because of her huge, baggy Protectors sweatshirt, with the symbol of the group on the front, curved and blue. And Lynn was easy to find because she was wearing her bobbing, horned Transforma headband. Transforma could shapeshift into any animal or alien the Protectors came across, though in her "human" form she always had red horns. And purple lips.

Kate stuffed her hands into the center pocket of her sweatshirt and gave Edie a little frown as she approached. Her freckled nose scrunched a little.

"Hey," Edie said. She wondered if Kate knew that Edie still read her fan fiction. She definitely didn't know that Edie still sketched it. Would she like it, if she knew? Or would she think it was pathetic?

Edie didn't know why she still kept up with the Protectors, or with Kate's work. She didn't know why she stored all her Protectors stuff in the closet instead of tossing it. Or why it was easier to let go of Kate herself than the thing that had brought them together.

"Hi!" Lynn said, a little too cheerfully. "Well . . . shall we? We want good seats, right?"

They went in, scanning their tickets at the entrance. Conversation was sporadic at best. It was like they were all leaving space for a fourth party to contribute, only that fourth party wasn't there. Amy had

always been critical of the comics, more so than Edie, Kate, or Lynn. Edie thought she didn't even *like* them, for a long time, before she saw Amy's bedroom, and all the posters tacked to the walls there, and the stack of Protectors-themed T-shirts in Amy's closet. It was just Amy's nature to pick at things.

They settled themselves in the middle of the theater, in the middle of the row. The floor was sticky under Edie's shoes. She'd smuggled a box of candy into the theater—chocolate-covered raisins, her favorite. She buried her fingers in the box, and Kate eyed her for a second before sticking out her hand, silently asking for some. Edie provided them automatically, her muscles remembering how to be Kate's friend even if the rest of her didn't.

"I'm excited to see how they portray the Charge," she said to Kate, across Lynn's body. Lynn was a good mediator, and she had trouble taking sides. Amy had started fights and Lynn had smoothed them over, time and time again. But Kate and Edie weren't having a fight now, not exactly.

Edie ran her fingers over the dark red velour that covered the seats, worn where most people's legs pressed against it, and watched the little screen as she waited for Kate to respond. It was so early the theater was playing trivia instead of coming attractions.

"I'm nervous about that," Kate said. "The budget wasn't that high for this movie. You know, because it's not a sure thing."

"Yeah, we all know ladyhero movies don't make money," Edie said, rolling her eyes. "Except, say, that Wonder Woman movie . . ."

"And *Black Widow*!" Lynn piped up, her horns bouncing on their springs.

"They're just looking at the facts," Edie said with false firmness. "Don't get so emotional about it, ladies. Are you PMSing, by the way?"

Kate laughed.

"Shh," Lynn said suddenly. "The lights are dimming."

And it all came back in a rush, that breathless feeling when all the expectations and hopes and fears formed over years

were balanced on a knife's edge. When you had loved something for so long and for so many reasons that all you wanted was for that love to expand inside you.

She clenched a hand around the armrest, and watched, forgetting about the chocolate-covered raisins spilling into her purse, and the tension that had driven her further and further away from Kate until they couldn't even speak to each other anymore, and the way Lynn chewed so loudly Edie could hardly hear the quieter lines.

She watched Vim and Vigor stumble out of uncertainty and embrace their heroism and save the city.

She watched them grow up together, then break apart, and come back together again for the sake of something greater than either of them was alone.

And in the climactic moments where it looked like Vigor might be lost in the power of the Charge, directing it to destroy instead of to heal, Edie locked eyes with Kate and smiled.

"And the part where Vim was double-fisting coffee cups with all those stacks of paper around?" Kate laughed.

"Classic Vim. Can't go anywhere without making a mess," Edie said, almost proud, for some reason. After all, Vim had been *hers*.

"The final act was a little fast, pacing-wise," Lynn said. "But I liked the rest. Wonder if it'll do well."

"Hope so," Kate said. "I really want a sequel."

"Yeah, me too," Edie said, a little wistful. By the time a sequel came out, they would all be in college, and what if she didn't find anyone to share the Protectors with there? Would she have to pretend like she was over it, like she did with Arianna?

Kate checked her phone. "It's still early. Want to go back to my place?"

"Sure," Edie agreed, though a second later, she regretted it. Lynn had that look on her face, the one that said she was about to say no.

"I have to head home," Lynn said. "I didn't finish my physics homework, and it's not like I'm acing that class."

Kate gave Lynn a knowing look that made Edie realize how little she knew about Lynn's life now. She had no idea if Kate or Lynn were acing their classes, or if either of them were dating anyone, or if they had had their first drink, their first grope, their first anything.

And Edie had already agreed to go to Kate's house. If she backed out now, it would be obvious that she didn't feel comfortable alone with Kate anymore.

"Um . . . meet you there?" she asked Kate.

"Sure," Kate said, sounding just as uncertain.

Edie couldn't help but think that everything would be easier if she could just say what was going on. *Look, you and I clearly aren't comfortable around each other without Lynn there, so maybe another time?* But that just wasn't what people did.

Edie was always running into the barriers between people, wishing they were easier to break.

Kate's house was stark and modern, pale floors and white walls and stacks of glass blocks instead of windows. When she got there, she walked straight to the kitchen, where she knew Kate would be, dumping popcorn in a bowl and rustling in her white refrigerator for another can of soda.

"Want one?" Kate asked her.

"No, thanks," Edie said. "Where are Dr. and Dr. Rhodes?" Her affectionate names for Kate's parents, one of whom studied brains and the other, history.

Kate's dad—the famous Dr. Russell Rhodes—invented the Elucidation Protocol, simulated reality technology that aided in clarity of thought and decision-making for people in high-stress fields. It essentially used extensive research, psychological and sociological principles, as well as personal beliefs, to reveal the likely outcomes of particular decisions through virtual reality. He had envisioned it being used to help world leaders make decisions, but it was the legal sector that had taken to it the most. It was currently used in prisons to rehabilitate criminals, and in crime prevention with high-risk populations.

"On a date." Kate's mouth twisted. "They do that now. They make out in the kitchen, too."

Edie grinned. Her own parents slept in separate beds these days, claiming that her mother's snores were the reason, but Edie knew that wasn't all.

"So." Kate turned her soda can around in a circle. "Did you notice the Haze cameo at the end of the movie?"

As if Edie could have missed the Haze cameo. Haze was the youngest superheroine in the Protectors, and the movie had set up her origin story, showing a teenage girl staring on from the crowd as Vim and Vigor claimed their victory over the supervillain.

"Haze" was what they had called Amy. She had been the youngest of the four of them, too.

"Yeah," Edie said. "Good casting, though. That red hair."

"Remember when Amy tried to dye her hair red in her bathroom, and stained the tub permanently?" Kate smiled at her soda can. "Her mom was *so mad*. . . ."

"Yeah, and it turned her highlights pink," Edie pointed out. "Which I could have told her would happen, if she had asked, but *no* . . ."

"You always were best at that kind of thing," Kate said. "I guess it makes sense you've gone pro."

Edie looked down at her clothes—nothing special, just red jeans and a blazer with a little pin on the lapel. A skull and crossbones, to match the ones on the toes of her flat shoes. But it was more stylish than Kate's baggy sweatshirt. "Are you referring to my outfit?"

"Yeah." Kate shook her head. Her freckled nose twitched. "Sorry, I . . . I think it's cool, that you know about all that stuff. I still remember the day my mom presented me with a hairbrush instead of a comb, like 'Oh, I guess this might be easier for you.'"

Kate's mother had a short, practical haircut, and the most makeup Edie had seen her wear was a dab of concealer under her eyes. But Kate's hair was wavy and thick, frizzing close to the scalp so it glowed when light shone through it, and she had the kind of long, curled eyelashes other people pined over. No need for mascara.

"I remember that, too," Edie said. "We were fourteen and the comb just broke in your hair."

She laughed, and so did Kate, and that was how they ended up in Kate's bathroom, with the makeup Edie kept in her purse spread over the counter and Kate perched on a stool with Edie standing in front of her, talking to her about eyeliner.

After giving up on the sparkly eye shadow ("If I wanted to look like New Year's Eve threw up on my face, I have a bag of confetti I could use," Kate had remarked. "Why do you have a bag of confetti?" Edie had asked, laughing.), Edie and Kate sat on stools in the kitchen, tossing popcorn into their mouths. Then Edie thought to check her phone, which had been on silent since she got home from school that day.

There were three missed messages.

Arianna: Don't leave me in suspense!

Chris: ???

Evan: Up for a smoke tomorrow during lunch?

Edie stared at Chris's question marks, and her heart began to pound. "???" was right.

She didn't know why it was so hard to make this decision—it was prom, after all, not life or death—but the thought of the way Evan's eyebrows would pinch in the middle, half disappointed and half critical, or the way Chris's eyes would avoid hers in the hallway again, as they had since the breakup, was just . . . too much. Right now, before she decided anything, all the different parts of her life were suspended in midair. And once she did, everything would come crashing down, she just knew it.

Kate must have seen the panic flash in her eyes, because she let the popcorn kernel fall on the floor and asked, "You okay, Vim?"

The casual use of the nickname—probably unintentional—made tears prick in Edie's eyes. And then she had an idea.

"Hey, you know that prototype your dad has in the basement?" she asked. "For the Elucidation Protocol? Do you think he would mind if we . . . used it?"

Kate raised her eyebrows.

"Let's see. Would my dad mind if I touched the thing he's always telling me not to touch under pain of death and the removal of my bedroom door?" She scratched her chin. "Yeah, Edie, pretty sure he would. Why?"

"I just . . ." Edie closed her eyes. "There's a decision I need to make, and it's kind of a big deal, and I just . . . I thought the EP could help."

"That is what it's designed for," Kate admitted. "Um . . ." She chewed her lip, the way she always did right before she suggested something stupid. This time was no exception. "Let's do it anyway."

Edie brightened. "Really?"

"Yeah, Dad's not going to be home until late," Kate said. She paused, tilting her head as she looked Edie over. "It really is important, right?"

Edie hesitated.

"Yeah," she said finally. "I wouldn't ask if it wasn't."

The prototype of the Elucidation Protocol was a little disappointing when you came face-to-face with it. The first time, Edie had narrowed her eyes and said to Dr. Rhodes, "This is it?" It looked like a headband with a bunch of wires attached to it, running along the floor to a little computer. The device wasn't the revolutionary part, Dr. Rhodes had explained. The substance that triggered the program was. He had made batches and batches of it, to the point that the other Dr. Rhodes, his wife, insisted he stop bringing it home, particularly when the protocol moved to its next stages and the original formula was no longer viable.

So she wasn't surprised when Kate plucked a vial of the stuff from a shelf in the—completely packed—closet of identical vials, without a second thought. She even *tossed* it to Edie, who caught it, thankfully. She sat in the padded chair—ripped across the seat from overuse—and buzzed with nerves as Kate arranged the wired crown atop her head like she was some kind of sci-fi prom queen.

"Wrap that heart monitor thing around your arm, will you?" Kate said. She was in Scientist Mode now. She had never been into science the way Edie was, but she was capable enough, growing up under her father's watchful eye. It was Edie, though, who knew how to attach the heart monitor to her arm so that it would pick up her pulse, who untangled the wires and made sure the leads were secured to her temples.

"You know the drill, but I'm going to give you the whole speech anyway, okay?" Kate said as she sat behind the computer to set up the program. "The protocol will run twice, once for each of the options you're considering. It doesn't see the future; it just helps you to see what *you* think would happen in each of two scenarios. The prototype is flawed in that it can't account for any other factors aside from the knowledge you yourself possess, though it does assist in clarity of thought."

Edie nodded. She knew all this. Her hand was getting sweaty around the vial of substrate. She was worried it would tremble when she brought it up to her mouth to drink, and Kate would see it, and know how terrified she was. About *prom dates,* of all things.

But it was more than that, wasn't it? Evan was intellectual, daring, opinionated. Chris was kind, openhearted, enthusiastic. And when she was with either of them, *she* was those things, too; she was more than she could ever be alone, like Vim and Vigor and the Charge. It was a choice between dates, sure, but it was also a choice between Edies.

Wasn't it?

"I'll cue you verbally to start the second phase," Kate said. "So, drink up, and it should set in after ten seconds. Don't be alarmed when your scenery shifts, it's perfectly normal."

Edie nodded, and tipped the vial's bluish contents into her mouth.

Edie twisted her arms behind her back to push up the zipper on her black dress. It was simple, hanging from off-the-shoulder straps and clinging just enough—not too much—to her belly and thighs. She tucked a stray curl into the twist at the back of her head, then, making sure that her little brother wasn't anywhere nearby, sniffed under each armpit to check that she had remembered deodorant.

"Edie!" her mother sang from the first floor. "There's a boy here for you!"

"Coming!" she crowed back. She checked her winged

eyeliner one last time in the mirror, stuffed a Band-Aid in her silver clutch in case her shoes gave her blisters, and made her way downstairs.

Evan waited by the door. He wasn't carrying a corsage, and she hadn't expected him to, but it was still vaguely disappointing, like he couldn't be bothered to do something silly even if it was just a nice gesture. But she pushed that thought aside as she went down the steps, particularly as his lips twitched into a smile.

He wore a black suit, white shirt, black tie. Classic. And at least he wasn't wearing flannel. His hair had just as much product in it as it usually did, and it looked so thick she wanted to bury her hands in it.

"Let me get a picture of you two!" Edie's mother said, and she rustled in her purse for her phone. Poking at it like it was a typewriter, she found her way to the camera app and held it up. Evan pulled Edie close to his side, grinning.

She smiled back, and with a click, the moment was captured.

After a hug that lingered a beat too long, Edie broke away from her mother and followed Evan to his old green Saab. She loved the way the car smelled, like tobacco and men's deodorant. She wondered what she would find if she opened the center console, and made a list of guesses. A tin of mints, a lighter with half the fluid gone. Maybe, if she dug deep, the stub of a joint, and a button from a winter coat. People's scraps said so much about them.

They didn't talk much on the way there, as Evan parked and

they piled into one of the buses with everybody else. Edie loved seeing all the people in their formalwear stuffed between bus seats, some of the skirts so big they fluffed up by a girl's face. Evan chose a seat in the back, next to an open window, and he sat a little closer to her than was strictly necessary.

"You didn't want to sit near your friend? What's her name?" Evan asked. "Arianna, right?"

"She went on the early bus—yep, it's Arianna," she said, inordinately pleased that he remembered Arianna's name. "You corrected her grammar once, remember?" she added on a whim, a little smile on her lips.

"Did I? God, she must hate me." Evan laughed. "It's a reflex. My mom used to make a horrible sound every time we made a grammar misstep. I think it was her attempt at classical conditioning."

"What was the sound?"

Evan's face contorted, and he let out a loud "EHH!" Like a warning buzzer mixed with an old car horn. There was a rustle of skirts as some of their classmates turned toward the sound.

Edie mimicked Evan's expression of horror. "She did that *every time*?"

"God forbid we used the word 'like' as a filler word," he replied sourly. "My parents split up when I was twelve, though, so her influence wasn't as strong after that. You know what they say about the formative years, though."

"They form you," Edie supplied. "You lived with your dad, then?"

"He's the responsible one," Evan replied, nodding. "So to speak. He hasn't noticed my unexcused absences yet, but I'm not complaining."

He was complaining, though, Edie knew. The same way she complained about her parents avoiding each other's eyes when they were in the same room together—by pretending it was better that way.

She wasn't sure where the question came from, but it was bubbling from her mouth. "Why did you want to be my friend, Evan?"

She had wondered more than once. And the answers she came up with ranged from *Because I wanted to get in your pants* to *Because your knowledge of cutting-edge neuroscience is downright alluring* and everywhere in between, but what he said surprised her anyway.

"You seemed as lonely as I was," he said, and he looked away, his hair tousled by the wind.

The bus rattled and rocked all the way to the Holiday Inn ballroom, which was decorated with different kinds of strings of lights, stars and roses and tiny lanterns. A folk-pop song with a twangy guitar was playing over the sound system, and there were a dozen round tables arranged next to the dance floor. A buffet table held deep trays of food, covered to keep them warm.

She spotted Arianna and her boyfriend, Jacob, already cuddled close at one of the tables, a plate of finger food between them. A hint of movement caught her eye on the side of the room, and she spotted Kate gesticulating wildly to Lynn. Edie blinked. Kate was wearing black pants and a glittery shirt that caught the light when she moved, and Lynn was in a red knee-length dress.

Kate's eyes found hers. Then looked away.

"Wow," Edie said. "This is a teen movie nightmare."

"You said it," Evan said. "I think I need a smoke. Want to?"

"A little early to bail, don't you think?" she said.

"I came, I saw, I prommed," he replied. "We can always come back. Come on, there's a place I want to show you."

They ended up a few blocks away, at the boardwalk. The smell of salt and seaweed was on the air, as well as the occasional whiff of cigarette smoke whenever the wind blew just so. The cigarette itself dangled from Evan's fingers like he was about to drop it, just like Edie's shoes dangled from hers by their little black straps.

He did put out the cigarette, then, smashing it against the inside of a little tin he kept in his jacket pocket. A second later she thought she saw him pop a mint into his mouth, but she couldn't be sure. She ducked her head to hide a smile, and followed him at his gesture. Then he was hopping off the boardwalk, drawing a gasp from her lips and a laugh from his own.

"Don't worry, there's a sandbar here at low tide," he said, and his pale hand stretched out around the boards beneath her. She set down her shoes, hiked up her skirt—all the while sparing a few choice words for boys who didn't understand how much harder it was to maneuver in a slinky dress than a pair of loose pants—and jumped down.

She splashed a little in the landing, but since her dress was black, it didn't really matter. She kept her skirt out of the sand, though, draping it over her elbow as she turned to face him. Yes, he had definitely eaten a mint—even from a foot away, his breath was fresh now, with a hint of tobacco.

"If we weren't in formalwear, I'd suggest we sit down and listen to the waves," he said. He ducked his head, and to her surprise, blushed a little. Or she thought he did—it was getting dark, so it was hard to tell. "Guess I didn't think this through very well."

"You know, it would probably be creepy if you had," she said, and he laughed, with less control than he usually had, so it came out like a bark.

And she realized, suddenly, that Evan—journal-carrying, smoking-behind-the-shed-on-school-grounds, pep-rally-ditching *Evan*—was nervous. That for all that he pretended to know himself and what he wanted, he was just as clueless about the whole thing as she was.

So she let her skirt drop to the sand, threw an arm around his neck, and tilted up on her bare toes to kiss him.

She felt his fingers digging into her waist, and the grains of sand between her toes, and the firm pressure of his mouth. Then, at the nudge of a tongue, parting, giving way, the tension thrumming through him releasing. Salt and mint and cigarette. Waves caressing the shore, and the moon now emerging, and she was exactly the daring girl she wanted to be.

"Second phase in five . . . four . . . three . . . two . . . one . . ."

Edie twisted her arms behind her back to push up the zipper on her red dress.

"I got it, don't dislocate anything," Arianna said, coming up behind her. She was already wearing a yellow gown that almost glowed against her brown skin. She had gathered her thick hair into a knot just behind her right ear, and there was a flower pinned there, just as bright as the dress.

Edie's friend zipped her up, and smiled at her reflection in the bedroom mirror. They picked Arianna's house for its huge staircase—perfect for prom pictures.

Edie had *tried* to buy a normal, simple dress, but Arianna had forbidden it. *This is one of the only times in your entire life that it will be okay to wear a huge monstrosity,* she had pointed out, and after a few repetitions, Edie agreed. Consequently, her red dress was a *gown,* with a full skirt.

And *pockets.*

She beamed when she moved in it and heard the layers swishing up against each other. Making sure her phone was secure in one of the pockets, she followed Arianna out of the bedroom. A group had gathered at the bottom of the grand staircase, all the boys in their tuxes and the girls in bright dresses of almost every color of the rainbow. They were Arianna's cross-country teammates, and Edie liked them, but didn't really know them. It didn't matter—she knew Arianna, and she knew Chris, who was laughing by the door with Arianna's boyfriend, Jacob.

When he spotted her, his face—if possible—lit up even more, and he broke off his conversation to go to her side.

"Nicely done, Robbins," he said.

"You too, Williams," she replied, making a show of looking him over. He did look good. Unlike the penguin-like boys around him, he was in a navy-blue tuxedo with black trim, his bow tie so straight it was like he had tied it with a level on hand. And he was holding a white wrist corsage. An orchid.

She grinned as he slipped it on her, then caught his hand, and squeezed.

"I see you're committed to this occasion," she said. "Corsage, nice suit . . ."

"When I was a boy I used to dream about my prom night. . . ." He folded his hands under his chin and gave an exaggerated blink. "And about the gal who would sweep me off my feet, et cetera."

She mimed throwing up.

"Really, though, my granddad always says cynicism is unattractive in a young person," he said a little more seriously. "Well, actually, he says 'What do you have to be cynical about, boy? The whole world is at your feet,' and something about a war, I don't know."

"Meanwhile, there's my mother, who started to warn me against bad prom-night decision-making and gave up halfway through," she replied. "Like, literally gave up. Sighed heavily and went into the living room."

Chris laughed. They took their place on the steps with

the other couples. He stood close behind her, wrapping an arm around her waist. They smiled, stiffly, for the first few shots, and when commanded to be silly, Edie put on a comically deep frown as Chris pretended to collapse against the banister.

Before pulling away, he bent closer to brush a kiss against her cheek. She flushed with warmth.

They piled into a white stretch limousine that took them—in a cloud of vapor from the smoke machine—to the high school, where they got on one of the buses instead. They rode in the back, raucous enough to get scolded multiple times by the chaperone. Edie's stomach ached from laughing so hard, and they weren't even at the prom yet.

When they arrived, she and Chris paused in the doorway to marvel at the strings of light that crisscrossed the ceiling, and the luminous gauze that made up the centerpieces of the tables. There wasn't a soul on the dance floor yet, though the lights were already low and the music was playing. So she knew what Chris was going to do before he did it.

He grabbed her hand and pulled her toward the dance floor. "Someone's gotta get this started!" he said by way of explanation, but she didn't need it. Her cheeks were hot as he pulled her into the empty space, and she felt the eyes of everyone in the room like fingers brushing over her, but then Chris was going through his repertoire of stupid dance moves, trying to get her to laugh with him: the cabbage patch, the shopping cart, the sprinkler . . .

Edie sighed, bobbed her head to the music, and pretended

to be holding a fishing pole. She cast her invisible line, and Chris became the fish, flapping wildly as she pulled him in. Then she fell against him, so embarrassed she couldn't help but bury her face in his shoulder. But it was all right, because in the middle of her spasm of humiliation, Arianna and all her friends had come to join them, and now she was camouflaged by a whole crowd of fools.

It took another song to get comfortable, and then Arianna was spinning in circles around her, and Jacob was dragging a handkerchief across his sweaty forehead, and Chris was trying to teach her how to do the electric slide, even though it didn't work with the music. She kept tripping over her skirt, and her legs were sticky with sweat, but it didn't matter, none of it mattered except how widely he smiled at her.

Sometime in the middle of one of those songs where they shouted commands at you—Edie's favorite, because she didn't have to think of her own moves—she spotted Kate at the edge of the dance floor, trying to coax Lynn to join her. Kate was in silver—no, not just silver, but a dress made of *duct tape* that wrapped around her from chest to knee. Lynn was in red, like Edie.

Edie caught Kate's eye, pointed at the duct-tape dress, and gave her a thumbs-up.

Kate gave her a confused look.

And Edie stepped to the left and turned, as commanded by the music.

The song slowed, and the lights went low, so only the starry strands glowed in a net above them. Chris's hands found her hips, and she put her arms around his neck. They swayed, leaning on each other to recover from the fever of the past few dances.

She touched her forehead to his, and he was sweaty, his skin radiating heat, but she didn't mind.

He had made her feel light, for once. So she tipped her chin up to kiss him. He cupped her cheeks, and they stopped swaying. She crushed the corsage against his chest, toying with the buttons of his shirt, with the perfectly straight bow tie.

This was it, she knew. The feeling people meant when they talked about love. And it was so easy to love him, so easy to love the person she was when he was around.

"You look happy," he said to her softly, over the hum of the music. "For a while, after the accident, it was like . . . like you didn't feel much of anything. And I didn't know what to do. But . . . it's nice to see you happy again."

It was nice to feel happy again.

But she couldn't get rid of the unsettling thought: *What happens when I stop being happy again?*

Kate did not count down her exit from the Elucidation Protocol. Edie jerked from the vision, startled to find herself sitting instead of standing, and wearing jeans instead of a red gown. She ran her hands over her arms, feeling bereft. Lost.

Such a weird thing to have in your basement, she thought as she looked around for something to anchor her. Along the far wall were bookcases stuffed with books, sometimes two rows deep. This was a house of curious people. Kate's parents didn't even mind her comic obsession. Her mother had called it a "feminist undertaking."

Kate stood in front of her, and ripped one of the wires away from Edie's forehead. Her movements were sharp, her brow furrowed. Edie blinked up at her as Kate eased the crown off her head and set it aside. Then Kate took a phone out of her back pocket and thrust it at Edie.

"Here. Take it, it wouldn't stop buzzing," Kate said. She folded her arms.

"What is it?" Edie said, still feeling out of it. Had she mumbled something while she was under the influence of the EP? Something about Kate?

"Oh no, this conversation can wait until you've checked your texts. Go ahead," Kate said.

Edie touched the screen, bringing up the last few text messages. They were all from Arianna.

Arianna: Well?

Arianna: Did you choose a boy yet?

Arianna: Tell me soon, because we need to go dress shopping together.

She looked up at Kate, still not sure what was going on.

"Tell me," Kate said, her voice shaking. "Tell me we didn't just break my father's rules, risk me getting in serious trouble, and potentially damage highly expensive equipment so you could *pick a prom date*."

"It's not . . ." But what? How could she explain that it wasn't about a prom date, wasn't about Evan or Chris or dresses or dances? How could she possibly tell Kate about the whirl of panicked thoughts chasing themselves through her brain every second of every day, and the deep ache she felt every time she thought about the future, the past, hell, even the present?

"God." Kate closed her eyes. "When you agreed to come tonight, I thought it was because you actually gave a damn about me still. That maybe we could be friends again. And now I find out you would take advantage of me like this, for something so . . . so *vapid* and shallow and—"

"You're so *judgmental*, God," Edie snapped. "If you're not ragging on me for liking makeup, you're insulting me for caring about prom? Well, excuse me for not waging some kind of eternal war against the Man!"

"You don't listen, do you?" Kate's eyes filled with tears. "I thought we could be friends again! And it's like you don't even think of me, don't even see me anymore, not since . . ." She blinked the tears away. "Do you even *like* Vim and Vigor anymore? Or did you just come so you could ask me for this?"

"*You're* the one who doesn't even make eye contact in the hallway," Edie said. "And you must not know me very well if you think I'm just some airheaded idiot who's agonizing over a prom dress."

"Just go, okay?" Kate shook her head. "Just go, and choose a boy, and go back to pretending I don't exist."

She turned and walked across the basement. Edie listened to her footsteps on the stairs, and above her head, as they crossed the living room. She heard a door close upstairs and knew that Kate would be in her room by now, probably playing music louder than she should, and wouldn't answer the door even if Edie pounded on it.

So Edie got her bag, put on her shoes, and left.

They had been the last ones at the funeral, Lynn, Kate, and Edie. They helped Amy's aunts clean up, then sat on the couch in the living room, sucking down the last of what Edie mentally referred to as the funereal punch. All day she had been suppressing the horrible urge to laugh. Everything was funny—the priest's hobbling gait as he went up to the pulpit, the face Amy's grandmother made when she cried, the off-balance way the pallbearers carried the casket.

She felt like some of the wires in her brain were crossed to trigger the wrong reactions at the wrong times. As people stood around weeping, she got so angry she thought she might explode, and excused herself. By the time she made it to the couch with Kate and Lynn, she was so exhausted from the wild swells of the wrong emotions that she was numb.

Then Lynn's parents came to pick her up, so it was just Kate and Edie, waiting for their rides together, and Edie still couldn't look Kate in the eye.

Kate put down her mug, her hand trembling, and said, in a voice so small and so broken Edie almost didn't believe it belonged to her friend:

"Do you think it's my fault?"

She knew why Kate was asking. Because it had been Kate's idea to drive to the 7-Eleven, and Kate who had been behind the wheel, and Kate who hadn't gotten out of the way of the drunk driver in time, and Kate whose whole body was shaking now.

Edie threw her arms around her best friend, held her tight, and forced herself to say, "No. Of course not."

But oh God, maybe she did, maybe she *did*.

That night Edie opened the Vim and Vigor folder on her tablet, and scrolled through the images one by one. Kate had been writing this most recent Protectors story for almost a year. It was longer than most books, and she updated it weekly on FandomWorks. Every time Edie thought about giving it up, she found something that made her hold on—a phrase she recognized, a revelation about a character, something small.

Then a few months ago, she discovered something bigger.

Kate had always teased Edie for being conventional in her "ships"—the couples she was most rooting for in fan fiction, even if they weren't together in canon. Kate was more interested in nontraditional interpretations of Vim and Vigor—Vim with other women (Transforma, mostly), and Vigor as asexual, or demisexual—and Edie liked to hear about those, too, curious about all the possibilities. (Though it had been difficult to explain to her mother why she had so many sketches of two women kissing on her tablet.)

But Edie always went back to Vim and Antimatter, the son of their evil nemesis. The early comics showed them potent in their hatred for one another, almost killing each other every now and then. But then Antimatter's mother had died, and he started to shift, and the passionate hate turned to attraction.

Enemies to lovers—one of Edie's favorite tropes.

And Kate had written it into her story.

Her Vigor was asexual, of course—that was Kate's favorite interpretation of all. But Vim and Antimatter were there, in her fic, the one she had been building for a year. It was almost like she was speaking directly to Edie.

That was when Edie started sketching again. Trying to talk back.

Edie paused on a drawing of Antimatter's gloved hand in Vim's slender one, their fingers twisting together as something exploded behind them. Maybe she didn't need to find the right words to say to Kate, or even any words at all.

Edie opened a blank email, and attached the Vim and Vigor folder. When it uploaded, she typed in Kate's email address and wrote "I'm sorry" in the subject line.

Sent.

It was prom night.

Edie twisted her arms behind her back to push up the zipper of her black skirt. It was high-waisted, hitting her right below her ribs, and made of a stiff material that disguised the cell phone and lipstick she carried in the pockets.

She leaned close to the mirror to check the border of her lipstick, which was a vibrant orange-red.

"So you're really set on that getup, huh," Arianna said from the doorway, her arms folded.

"Not much choice now, is there?" Edie smiled a little. "Come on. Let's go make precious memories."

There were strings of lights across the ceiling, just as she had imagined during the Elucidation Protocol, but none of them were shaped like stars. Instead, they were your standard Christmas light variety, little and twinkling and white. And the centerpieces on the round tables were just white flowers, lilies and carnations. Kind of hideous, actually.

Edie stood in the doorway and tucked her hands into her skirt pockets. She was scanning the hotel ballroom, at her leisure, watching Chris and his date—one of the cross-country girls, a short, sweet junior named Tonya—do the shopping cart, shoulder-to-shoulder. Evan was nowhere to be found, probably smoking under the boardwalk, if he had come at all.

Arianna turned back, her arm still looped around Jacob's elbow. "You coming?"

Edie waved her on.

Then she spotted them, standing at the edge of the dance floor, and she remembered the text she'd sent to Lynn and Kate a few days after the incident at Kate's house.

Edie: Protectors reunion at prom? ♥ Vim

She unzipped her leather jacket and tossed it over the back of a chair. Underneath it she wore a garish purple T-shirt with an illustration of Vim on it. The superheroine was flying through the air, her cape rippling behind her and her fist outstretched, jagged energy lines radiating from her body.

Across the room, Lynn spotted her and waved. She was wearing her Transforma horns and an acid-green dress that clashed horribly with them. She looked like a bottle of radioactive waste, and her lips were dark purple.

Kate turned, and when Edie recognized the Vigor costume for what it was, she almost cried with relief, because it meant Kate had forgiven her. From the back, the costume just looked like a rippling black coat-dress, but from the front, that bright red bustier was unmistakable. As was the sparkly red eye shadow on Kate's eyelids.

They looked insane. Ridiculous. And fantastic.

She crossed the room just as a fast song started playing. When she was close to Kate and Lynn, she struck the classic

Vim pose, and all three of them laughed.

"Look, I brought something," she shouted over the music. And she took a tiny picture of Amy out of her pocket. It was attached to a Popsicle stick, and decorated with the neon-yellow Haze headdress. And glitter.

"That is . . ." Lynn started, eyebrows raised. ". . . dark," she finished. "Very dark sense of humor you've got there, Edie."

But Kate was laughing. "Oh God, she would have loved it."

Edie grinned, and put it away. She knew it was weird. She hadn't really brought it for them. She brought it because she thought it might feel good to remember Amy. And terrible. She knew it would feel terrible to remember, too, but sometimes good and terrible could coexist, right? They had to. The same way you could be happy and sad at the same time.

People were big, and strange, and complicated. So she couldn't have chosen to spend this night with Evan, who only liked her when she was lonely, or Chris, who only liked her when she was happy. She had chosen Kate, who just liked *Edie*.

Kate, who Edie didn't blame for the accident, then. Not even a little.

"Let's go," she said. "I love this song."

ARMORED ONES

TWO STORIES OF SHOTET METTLE

I
TEKA

My mom had taught me never to refuse food or drink at a person's house, but when it came to the Storyteller's tea, I always wanted to forget my manners. It was sickly sweet and floral, like drinking perfume. It even *looked* like perfume, a transparent light purple.

I swallowed it in a big gulp, which turned out to be a mistake, because the Storyteller only poured me another cup. In front of me was a mismatched tea set, one cup silver; another, white; a third, yellow and chipped along the rim.

"I was pleased to hear from your mother," the Storyteller said. "Even through an envoy, I felt like I could hear her voice."

I knew the Storyteller because he had been helping people escape Shotet—and the tyranny of the dictator Lazmet Noavek, and later his son, Ryzek—for longer than I had been alive. And one of those people had been my mother, Zosita Surukta. She had to flee to escape execution, a sentence issued by the sovereign of Shotet himself for the crime of teaching a language other than Shotet to Shotet children. The Storyteller had found her a place on a transport ship bringing goods to the city. She had stowed away between sacks of offworld grains.

When Ryzek Noavek found out she was gone, he had my brother killed and my right eye cut out. It was bobbing in a jar in the Weapons Hall at Noavek manor.

"You must have a better imagination than me," I said. "All I hear when she writes is instructions."

I sat on the floor with a low, square table in front of me. The Storyteller's house was packed with little things. Fragments of glass hung from strings in front of the window, and when the sun shone through them, they cast spots of colored light on the opposite wall.

"You mustn't be too hard on her," he said, rubbing a hand over his shaved scalp. "She has to keep herself safe."

"Yeah, I know."

Someone knocked on the door, and the Storyteller got up to answer. I wasn't here to meet him, after all.

The Storyteller stood back to let the woman in. Her hair was a dull brown and tucked behind her ears. She was short, but somehow, she didn't seem small. Her clothes were fine enough, but simple, suggesting a comfortable amount of money, but not status.

Her name was Otega. I didn't know much else about her, except that she could train me to complete my mission:

I was going to kill Cyra Noavek, sister of the sovereign of Shotet. Better known as "Ryzek's Scourge."

"Your mother told me you're eager to be a renegade," she said to me, lifting a teacup to her lips. "But that your anger is a hindrance to you."

I decided, then, that I didn't like Otega.

"My mom's never had her eye cut out," I retorted.

"I take it that means you don't agree with her?" Otega said. She sat across the table from me, the tea set between us. She had chosen, of all the available cups, the chipped yellow one.

"My anger makes me focused on what's necessary, which is eliminating the Noaveks from power," I said, with heat. "I don't care about anything as much as I care about that. How is that a liability for a renegade?"

Otega raised her eyebrows. "For one thing, it makes you hostile in response to simple questions."

"I don't want to talk about my feelings," I said. "I want to get ready for my mission. If you can't help me with that, then we're both wasting our time."

"Well, perhaps I should tell you my credentials, then," she said. "I have worked in Noavek manor for twenty seasons. I helped raise Cyra Noavek, and tutored her until she became too skilled for me. I have been working to remove the Noaveks from power for longer than you've been alive." She tilted her head. "Do you think I can help you with your mission, Teka?"

I stared at her.

"Honestly?" I said after a few moments. "I think *you* should be the one to kill Cyra Noavek, not me."

Otega smiled. "My religious convictions are something of an obstruction."

"But helping me figure out how to kill her, that's not an obstruction?" I said. "Seems like following the letter of a law and not the spirit to me."

She pursed her lips, and set her teacup down. The Storyteller sat in the corner, sanding down the edge of a wood carving. He shifted the sandpaper back and forth in a consistent rhythm, rocking with the motion. It looked to me like he was meditating.

"Your mother called in a debt." Otega's voice was clear, and her eyes steady. So why did I feel like this was a confession? "And I have to repay her. That's all this is."

A debt was something I could understand. Not feelings, not religion—something straightforward, like the wires and devices I spoke to with my hands, using my currentgift. All they knew was their own function, and whatever kept them doing it. That was all I really needed to know from Otega, and all I needed to know about myself, too.

"Okay," I said. "What's next?"

My hair was wrapped in a gray scarf, to keep me from getting noticed. There was blond hair—not uncommon in Shotet—and then there was Surukta blond, which was so pale it was almost white, and tended to draw attention. My eyepatch, too, was distinct, so I had to put in my glass eye and comb my hair so it fell across the right side of my face. I was not supposed to draw attention to myself in the kitchens of Noavek manor.

Otega was there, laughing with one of the cooks as she folded linens. She had told him I was a niece of hers, sent to Voa to work, and he hadn't questioned it. My false name was Keza. I was dressed in Otega's clothes: a gray shirt with a vest over it, tucked into dark blue trousers, and black calf-high boots. The fabric was soft, but the clothes were loose enough that they almost blurred my figure, making me more forgettable.

"Keza, how are you at changing bed linens?" Otega said.

"Good enough," I said. "Why?"

"You're going to help me change out the linens in the west corridor. Wash your hands."

I had been chopping roots for the cook's stew. I washed my hands in the deep metal sink in the corner, then Otega piled my arms high with linens and led the way into the hidden hallways of Noavek manor.

She explained the marking system at the end of each hallway to me, and assured me that I would get used to maneuvering in the dark—everybody did. I was less worried about that and more worried about how long I would be in Noavek manor. Long enough to learn the hallways? Long enough to think of this as my *actual job*?

When she pulled back a wall panel, we were in the west corridor, on the second floor—also known as Cyra Noavek's wing. Fear buzzed in my chest. I wanted Cyra Noavek dead, sure, but I knew she was dangerous, and I didn't want to be discovered. I kept my head down as Otega led the way down the hall.

She stopped at the first door on the left, which was open. The room within was small, with an apothecary station on the left side packed with ingredients and tools. I recoiled when I saw the half-chopped currentflower on the counter. Otega grinned.

"He's basically immune to them," she said.

"Who?"

"The Kereseth boy."

"He lives here? Why?"

She was stripping the little bed across from the apothecary station of its sheets. There was a pile of pillows in the corner of the room. It looked like Kereseth had thrown them there in his sleep.

Everyone knew who Akos Kereseth was. Kidnapped from the land of our enemies, Thuvhe, with his brother; fated to die serving the family Noavek; trained with the Shotet army outside of the city; and now, apparently, resident of Noavek manor, for some reason.

"There are some things you don't know about Miss Noavek's currentgift," Otega replied. "It takes as much as it gives. And Kereseth's own gift . . . relieves things. Come along."

She led me down the hallway, past a large, empty room—"for training," Otega explained—and a huge bathroom—"for guests"—to a closed door on the right. She knocked, and a clear, feminine voice called out, "Come in."

Otega leaned in close to me, and whispered, "If you can't keep your head in this room, you can't handle your mission. Understand?"

I nodded, and followed her in.

And then I was in the same room as Cyra Noavek.

The blunt instrument Ryzek used to torture his enemies.

People said she was mad. Barely capable of forming coherent sentences. They said she could kill with a touch. That she relished it. That she frothed at the mouth like a rabid dog. That she was every bit as evil as her father had been.

It was dim inside the room—which was large enough to house half a dozen people rather than just one. All the blinds were closed, and the only light came from a floating projector. The monster herself stood facing the wall above the fireplace, watching the projected footage, which seemed to be of a hand-to-hand fight in some kind of arena.

I couldn't see her, at first, as my eyes adjusted to the light. I could tell that she was tall, with an athletic build, her thighs thick and her bare arms ropy with muscle. But when the footage lit up brighter—zooming closer to the fighters—I got a glimpse of her face.

I should have known she would be beautiful. Full lips and a stately nose; dark, focused eyes and elegant hands. But then a patch of dark, spidery veins sprawled over her cheek, and she flinched—as if her deadly currentgift hurt her.

Otega snapped her fingers at me, and I remembered myself, rushing over to the bed with the linens. She had already taken the sheets off the mattress and the pillowcases. My hands shook as I unfolded the fitted sheet and tried to spread it across the bed. Otega clicked her tongue at me and took it from me so she could do it instead.

"To what do I owe this honor?" Cyra said. Her voice was low, for a woman. "You haven't changed my sheets in seasons, Otega."

I could have sworn she didn't notice us come in.

"Just helping out one of the others," Otega said. "What are you watching?"

Her familiarity was surprising to me, but then, she had

tutored Cyra from her childhood, hadn't she? Maybe they were friendly. It seemed at odds with the image of Cyra Noavek in my mind—taciturn, cruel, and impatient. Someone capable of murder.

After all, she had killed my uncle, Uzul Zetsyvis.

His daughter, Lety, had told me what happened. That Cyra had put her hands on Uzul, at her brother's command, and tortured him senseless. That he had been unable to get rid of the pain, afterward, and had taken his own life. That Lety had sent a message to Cyra, telling her to mark the loss—mark my uncle Uzul's life—on her arm.

I couldn't tell if she had listened—a forearm guard covered her left arm from elbow to wrist.

"A demonstration from last year's Festival," Cyra said. "Ryzek asked me to fight Vas for the entertainment of the soldiers. I wanted to study it—I'm teaching Akos."

"Out of the goodness of your heart?"

Cyra snorted, which made Otega smile.

"He's making me painkillers," Cyra said. Another black vein shot down her right arm, from shoulder to wrist, and then spread in four branches down each finger. Cyra flinched again, and shook out her hand. "They're helpful. It's a fair exchange."

I looked from Cyra to the footage. In it, she stood in a practice arena—similar to the one on the Sojourn ship—with her hair tied back and her hands up by her face. Across from her was Vas Kuzar, his hair shaved on one side, bruises marking his arms. I nearly shuddered at the sight of him, Ryzek's constant companion, who couldn't feel pain.

Black lines spread across Cyra's skin in a dense web, and her entire body contorted before pulling in on itself. She stifled a moan.

In the footage, she was also covered in the black lines of her currentgift, but she was moving, sidestepping Vas and hooking her leg around his to trip him. He recovered, and delivered a wide punch—which she ducked under, and shifted back to punch him hard in the side. He grinned, making a grab at her; she twisted away, escaping him.

I forgot about the linens as I watched them gain momentum. They shifted forward and back, their feet fast, their bodies bending, twisting, tensing and releasing. It was like watching a dance, except the dancers kept colliding, all elbows and knees, fists and feet, bloody and bruised.

I had been practicing combat since before my mother's exile, and since then, I had doubled down on the exercise with a ferocity that alarmed most of the renegades I sparred with. I had made huge leaps forward in skill. Only a handful of the others could best me.

But one thing was distressingly clear: I was not as good as Cyra Noavek.

"Who won?" Otega asked. She snapped her fingers at me, and I tried to focus, arranging the pillows at the head of the bed.

"It was a draw," Cyra said, tilting her head as she watched. More currentshadows, these sprawling across her throat, like a hand, choking her. She stopped talking, closing her eyes instead and breathing through her nose. Then she continued, once the currentshadows moved on. "He wasn't getting hurt, and I wasn't getting tired, so Vakrez just told us to stop after a while."

"I guess you're evenly matched."

"Without his currentgift, he's above average at best," Cyra said, her brow furrowed. "He doesn't know how to think."

"We're all done," Otega said. "Let some light in eventually, would you? It's stuffy in here."

Cyra grunted a little in response. I followed Otega out of the room and down the hallway. As we passed Kereseth's room, I spotted him at the counter, handling the currentflower with his bare hands. He was tall, too, with skin as fair as mine, and deft hands that chopped in perfect increments.

Once Otega and I were in the hidden hallways again, and the wall panel was back in place, she turned to me. I could barely see her in the dark, only finding her face by the gleam of her eyes.

"What did you learn?" she said.

"What?"

"I didn't sneak you in here so you could change sheets, Surukta," she snapped. "Tell me what you learned."

"I'm not as good as she is," I said. "Not even close. None of us are."

"And?"

"And . . ." I couldn't think of what else was relevant to my mission, except maybe that Otega wanted me to know my enemy, generally. So I decided to stick to the hard facts: "Her currentgift causes her pain."

"*Constant* pain," Otega clarified. "Go on."

"She's observant. She knew you had come in even though she didn't look at you or acknowledge you. She's tall—a head and shoulders taller than me. Strong, to be sure. Beautiful. Focused. And . . . surprisingly casual with a servant, even one she's known for a long time."

"When she was a child, she refused to respond when I called her by any honorific," Otega said, nodding. "You handled yourself poorly. You couldn't focus on your task and observe her at the same time, you stopped to stare, you seemed overwhelmed by the experience overall. It's lucky for you that she was so focused on something else, or she would have noticed how strange you were acting in an instant."

"You can't expect me to just pretend she's not who she is," I snapped. "She's *Ryzek's Scourge*. It's a little distracting to suddenly be in the same room as her with only a few moments' warning!"

"You're so eager to be a renegade." Otega snorted a little. "But the truth is, you're a little girl with a grudge."

"It's not a little girl's grudge!" I snapped. "She *killed my uncle*. Her brother—"

“I do not care,” Otega snapped. “If you are discovered, you will be tortured, interrogated, and executed.”

She grabbed my arm, and pulled me close.

“This is what your mother meant when she said your anger was a hindrance,” she said in a low, harsh whisper. “It makes you a goddamn fool. And if you want to live long enough to complete your mission, you’ll stop wallowing in your hurt and grow a brain.”

She released me, grabbed what remained of the linens from my arms, and started down the hallway.

I spent the next week in Noavek manor, carrying laundry back and forth. Bed linens, towels, clothes, the place was stuffed full of so much fabric I thought I might drown in it, choked by pillowcases.

I spent the next week learning about Cyra Noavek. Her bedroom, I discovered, had no personal touches at all. It looked no different than the empty guest rooms in Noavek manor. I had no regard for her privacy, so when I collected her laundry, if the room was empty, I opened the cabinets in her spacious quarters and looked inside. I found trinkets from past scavenges: defunct Tepessar coins from a past currency; a single plate earring from Essander, stamped with concentric circles; a spinning top from Zold, coated with the planet’s trademark gray dust.

Another drawer held relics of Cyra’s late mother, Ylira Noavek. Not clothes and jewelry—though Cyra had some of those, too—but notes scribbled on scraps of paper in loopy handwriting, small vials of perfume, a silk handkerchief with a fenzu stitched into it. And beneath it, a printed picture of a child Cyra, sitting on her mother's lap. Ylira was smiling down at her daughter, and Cyra was smiling back. They didn't look anything alike.

As for the young woman herself, she was nearly always in the training room, sometimes with Akos, and sometimes without. I didn't dare to stop and watch them from the hallway, but once, when I went to change the sheets, there was a book on Cyra's bed. A book on elmetahak, the oft-forgotten text on Shotet strategic thinking in combat. She had made notes in the margins about Akos. *Loses his focus often, seems to coincide with bouts of insomnia. Teach meditation techniques?* And: *Leaves left side unguarded; may want to supplement armor accordingly.* The notes became more detailed the farther ahead in the book they were, and while they were always about combat, I started to wonder if they reflected a certain amount of . . . tenderness. You didn't watch someone that closely unless you cared about them.

On the seventh day that I found myself working in the manor, I walked into the kitchen and Otega was just standing at the counter, staring at her hands.

"You all right?" I said.

"Come," she said without looking at me, and she led the way into the hallway behind the wall.

This time, she didn't lead me up to the western part of the manor where Cyra Noavek lived. She reached back for my wrist as she took me down a complicated route on the first floor. Then she stopped, and crouched before a wall panel, drawing it carefully back, one sliver at a time.

She gestured for me to crouch there, too, and I did, putting my eye up to the narrow space she had created in the wall. I saw a sparse room awash in greenish light, and recoiled, my stomach turning.

I knew this room.

I knew it.

I clapped a hand over my mouth, and sat back, fighting for control of my breathing. I heard Ryzek Noavek's voice in my mind. *And to you, girl, I will give mercy*. The glass eye felt suddenly too big for its socket; I resisted the urge to claw it out. *I will leave you with your life . . . but not without a reminder.*

Otega's hands were on my head, her voice whispering in my ear. "I'm sorry, I'm sorry. I forgot. I'm sorry." Her palm pressed flat to my back, and moved in a slow circle, as my mother's had done when I was sick as a child. It brought me back to myself. I trembled a little, but my breaths evened out, and I took my hand away from my mouth.

"Do you want to go?" she asked me.

I shook my head. I sat forward on my knees, and looked through the gap in the wall again.

I forced myself to focus. Not on the greenish light, but on my target, on Cyra Noavek, standing at the foot of the dais in full armor. Earned armor. Up near the wall of weapons was Ryzek Noavek, that pale pillar of a man. I felt a surge of revulsion at the sight of him, at the flint of his voice.

". . . She found ways to avoid physical altercations,

acknowledging her weakness. You should be more like her, sister. You are an excellent fighter. But up here . . ." He tapped his head. "Well, it's not your strength."

I frowned. I was the future assassin of Cyra Noavek, but even I knew that wasn't the case. Cyra's strength in combat was in strategy more than physical skill.

"You gave Kereseth a weapon? You took him through the tunnels? You slept through his escape?"

I looked up at Otega, who was leaning over to watch above me. She nodded at me.

"He drugged me," Cyra said.

I thought of the apothecary station. It would be simple for him to drug her.

"Oh? And how did he do that?" Ryzek smirked. "Pinned you down and poured the potion in your mouth? I don't think so. I think you drank it, trustingly. Drank a powerful drug prepared by your enemy."

"Ryzek—" she choked out.

"You almost cost us our *oracle*. And why? Because you're foolish enough to let your heart flutter for the first painkiller who comes around?"

I couldn't see her face. But I knew by her sagging posture that he had struck a nerve.

"You can't blame him for wanting to rescue his brother," she said shakily, "or for wanting to get out of here."

"You really don't get it, do you? People will always want things that will destroy us, Cyra. That doesn't mean we just let them act on what they want."

He pointed, and for a horrible moment I thought he was pointing right at me. But he was just ordering her to one side of the dais.

"Stand over there and don't say a word. I brought you here to watch what happens when you don't keep your servants under control."

Whatever nerve he had struck seemed to have activated her currentgift. Currentshadows raced all over her body, making her clutch herself, face contorted.

Ryzek's Scourge. Shotet's living nightmare. The monster who had tortured my kind uncle until he was in enough pain to seek release by ending his life. I thought I would delight in watching her suffer.

But I had seen her as a child on a mother's lap, as a sister berated by her brother, as a girl with a crush. She had become a person to me, not a monster, and though I didn't forgive her for what she had done, I also didn't relish her pain.

I sat back on my heels.

Was that what Otega wanted me to learn? And if so . . . why? Would it make it any easier to complete my mission?

"We must go," Otega murmured in my ear. I didn't protest. I didn't want to see what would come next anyway—what torments Ryzek had devised for Akos Kereseth. So I stood, and together Otega and I walked back to the kitchen.

The next day I didn't go to Noavek manor. I stayed home to pack my things for the sojourn, our rite of traveling the galaxy and descending on a planet to scavenge. The most sacred of Shotet rituals. As a mechanic, I was needed aboard the sojourn ship earlier than most people, to make sure everything was running smoothly. I had told Otega as much, and she had made excuses for me with the manor staff, saying her sister had gotten ill, and her young niece Keza had to go home to care for her.

Jorek Kuzar showed up that night, and there was a bruise at the corner of his eye. I didn't ask about it, because I knew where it had likely come from. Jorek's father, Suzao, was not a patient man. Or a good one.

Jorek was from a family of Noavek loyalists. His cousin was Vas Kuzar, Ryzek's closest companion. He had turned against the Kuzars and joined the renegades at a young age, and he often turned up at my doorstep, hungry and saying nothing of where he'd just been.

"Need something to eat?" I asked. "I have . . . crackers."

He was already opening one of the kitchen cabinets. I lived with a cousin and his wife, and they worked at night, so we were rarely home at the same time. We were related through my father, who had died when I was a baby. He, like me, had had a talent for machines, though his was unrelated to his currentgift. His arm had gotten caught in the gears of one, and he had lost so much blood while he waited for a doctor to show up that he had died stuck there.

It had been his right arm. The same side as my eye.

"Your cousins here?" Jorek said, his mouth full of cracker.

"First of all, don't get crumbs on the floor, we already have a pest problem," I said. Everyone did, in this part of the city—the outer rim, where poor people lived packed together in these little apartments. Our kitchen had a single burner, two cabinets, and a table just long enough for two of us to sit at once. My room was actually a hall closet with a bed crammed into it.

"Second, no, they're gone."

"And nothing is . . ." He tapped his ear, and pointed up at the ceiling. Asking if there was any reason not to talk about renegade business.

I shook my head. I would know if there were any devices in the walls. It was always worth checking—my mother was in exile, after all. The Noavek regime would have its eye on me for as long as I was alive.

"Okay. How's mission prep going?" he said. "Heard a Dormant was helping you."

Dormant was the term for a renegade who didn't regularly attend meetings, usually because they were on some kind of long-term, sensitive mission. Otega was one. My aunt Yma was another. I hadn't spoken to her in seasons, and that wasn't likely to change anytime soon. Most renegades didn't know what a Dormant's mission was, and we weren't allowed to ask, or risk contacting them in any way.

"Yeah," I said. I worried my bottom lip between my teeth. I had been feeling strange since yesterday. Strange about Otega.

"I know I'm not supposed to tell you who it is," I said, "but I could really use some insight."

Jorek pulled out one of the rickety chairs at the kitchen table and sat sideways in it, one arm slung across the back.

"You can trust me," he said. "I won't tell anyone."

"I know," I said. "Okay, well—in all your fancy Kuzar time

lying on silk and eating rare delicacies, did you ever meet a woman named Otega?"

"Only fabric woven by the hands of servants for the fanciest of Shotet," Jorek said. "Don't be silly."

"Forgive me, I am but a lowly commoner." I grinned.

"Yeah, I know Otega. She was Cyra's tutor, and she works in the manor." His eyebrows popped up in surprise. "She's a *renegade*?"

"No. Maybe. I don't know." I pulled out the chair next to him and sat. Our knees bumped together under the table, and I angled myself away so we could both sit without being on top of each other. "Why is that so surprising?"

Jorek shrugged. "She's been working for the Noaveks for a long time. She practically raised Cyra. And now she's helping you learn how to kill her? I don't know, it's just . . . surprising."

"Okay, that's the thing." I planted one elbow on the table and leaned toward him. "I'm not entirely convinced she's helping me learn how to kill her. I think she's trying to get me to screw it up."

Jorek frowned. "But your mom wouldn't set you up with someone she wasn't sure of, would she?"

"My mom thinks she knows everything, but what can she really know about a woman from a forest in Ogra?" I rolled my eyes. "She hasn't even lived here in five seasons. The places she knew, the people she knew—they've changed."

"Have you tried asking her?"

"My mom?"

"No. Otega." He scratched at the patchy beard he was

growing on his chin. I had teased him about it for weeks when it first started coming in, poking a finger into all the bald patches. "Confront her. Even if she lies about it, you might be able to tell just by her reaction."

"That," I said, "is an idea worth half a box of crackers."

"I like to earn my keep," Jorek said, popping another one in his mouth.

I ran a finger along my hairline, checking that the scarf was in place. It was. I had bundled my hair into a tight knot and wound the scarf around it to disguise it, and the only hint of my Surukta blond came from my eyebrows, so pale they disappeared.

I went through the back gate, nodding to the guard the same as I had the last week. He asked my name and checked it against the picture he had on file, then deactivated the lock and let me in. I felt the faint whir of machines in the air, saying hello to me through my currentgift. *Not now,* I thought, though I wanted to say hello back.

Otega wasn't in the kitchen when I walked in, but I told the cook I would wait, and helped him put away the spices he had gotten out for lunch.

"I thought you had already gone home, Keza," Otega said to me when she returned to the kitchen.

"I'm leaving today," I said. "But I need to talk to you first. Somewhere private."

"Okay." Otega glanced at the cook. "Let's go to the storeroom."

I followed her down a short flight of steps to the storeroom, where all the produce was kept. The room was insulated and cold, like a refrigerator. I touched one of the walls, searching with my currentgift for the familiar titters and buzzes of recording devices and sights. I found sights watching us—not a surprise, because the Noaveks were bound to guard against theft—but nothing listening. Good.

The room had once been a basement, so it was half underground, with slim windows near the ceiling to let in some light. Still, it was dim enough that shadows found the creases in Otega's skin, hints of a hard life. Tables littered with produce filled the room, and we stood between two of them, facing each other. I folded my arms.

"What kind of game are you playing?" I said to her.

"I have no idea what you mean," Otega said.

"You're supposed to be helping me prepare for my mission. Which, in case you had forgotten, involves *killing Cyra Noavek*." I kept the last few words quiet, looking over Otega's shoulder to make sure no one stood at the door. "So why don't you tell me how, exactly, you've been doing that?"

Otega's mouth was a firm line. Her posture mirrored mine, arms folded, feet planted. And she wasn't answering.

"I'm waiting," I said.

"My intention was to diminish your anger by revealing to you that your enemies are people, not monsters," Otega said. "It has made you more level-headed, which will help you with your mission."

I thought about that for a moment. And then I shook my head.

"Try again," I said. "I don't believe you."

"It doesn't really matter what you believe, because it's the truth."

"No. The truth is, you've known Cyra Noavek since she was a child. You know she's in constant pain. You know that Ryzek Noavek is cruel to her. You know that she is capable of tenderness. *You know her,* and you love her." I scowled at her. "You don't want me to kill her, but you had to pretend to help me, because of whatever my mother is holding over your head. So why don't you tell me what that is, and we can have a real conversation about this instead of this goddamn nonsense?"

"No," Otega said, her voice wobbling. She swallowed hard.

"No matter what you do, or what you say, I am going to kill her," I said, leaning in close. "You succeeded in making me more level-headed, but I am not doing this because I want to commit murder, I'm doing it because it *needs to be done.* The Noaveks are a blight on Shotet. When they're gone, we'll be able to build something new. Surely you must realize that."

“Nothing good can be built on the bodies of innocents,” Otega snapped.

“She’s not an innocent. She is responsible for what she does, the same as anyone else,” I said. “Just like you are, for whatever you did that my mom is using as blackmail. You think if you do this, your debt will be repaid? That’s not how it works. That’s why we tattoo our losses on our skin. Because some things can’t be erased.”

Otega blinked, and just like that, her eyes were full of tears.

“Someone told Ryzek Noavek how to find you and your brother, after your mother fled,” Otega said.

I knew, then, what she would say. I knew, and it pierced me. Ran me right through.

“That person was me,” she finished.

I closed my eye.

It had taken two men to hold me down, their hands rough on my shoulders, and a third to steady my head, one hand on my forehead, the other under my chin. *Keep your eyes open,* the fourth said. *Or we’ll take your eyelid as well as your eye.*

And I had.

Stared into the point of the blade as it came down.

I knew, then, that I could do what needed to be done. Because I had already proved that I could. I had been steady in the face of horror. I had borne the death of my brother and the loss of my mother. I always did what I had to, when it was really important. I could count on myself.

I opened my eye and looked at her.

“Do you know what this tells me?” I said. “That you value

the life of Cyra Noavek, born into privilege—a person, yes, but still a person who chooses to torture and kill—over my life. Which is exactly the Shotet problem. Noavek lives are more important than anyone else's, and it's time for that to end."

I pulled down the lower eyelid of my right eye, and felt along the bottom of the prosthetic until I could wedge my finger beneath it. I popped out the disc, and with my free hand, grabbed Otega's wrist so I could deposit the false eye in her palm. She recoiled, but I held her fast.

"No more Noaveks," I said.

I left her standing there.

A week later, I stood in the audience of the arena on the sojourn ship, and watched as Cyra Noavek killed my cousin, Lety Zetsyvis.

I didn't flinch.

I was ready.

2
AKOS

"As I have told you a dozen times now," Vakrez Noavek said to him, "I am not going to waste anyone's time with this."

Akos had walked into the room determined to stay calm. To prove to the commander that he wasn't some thin-skinned Thuvhesit boy. But instead, what burst out of his mouth was a petulant "It won't *be* a waste of time!"

He was there to request the Shotet Rite of Armor, in which a candidate went head to head with an Armored One—the most dangerous creature on their planet—and either killed it or died in the attempt. The rite required three observers and the sponsorship of an authority figure. In this case, that authority would have to be Commander Vakrez Noavek of the Shotet army. Akos had asked for it for months, and he had been denied every time.

Vakrez's husband, Malan, was sitting in the corner of the room with a book in his lap. At Akos's outburst, he shook his head, his lips twitching into a smile.

Vakrez looked up from the letter he was writing. "Control yourself, Kereseth."

Akos spoke the word of calm into his mind—the Shotet word *kyendat*, which he had spent hours training into his subconscious, along with relaxed muscles and a sharp focus on his surroundings. At the sound of it, he felt his frustration ebb away. Someday he wouldn't need the word, his body would just listen to him better—or so his Shotet lieutenant said. But for now, it helped.

"I'm sorry, sir," Akos said, steady. "But I know the rules. Any soldier who asks for this rite is supposed to get it."

"You are not a soldier," Vakrez said. "You are a prisoner of the sovereign of Shotet. Or have you forgotten?"

The anger he felt for Ryzek Noavek was no momentary flare of frustration, nothing that could be controlled with *kyendat*. It simmered deeper than anything he'd ever felt, a pool of acid in the pit of his stomach that never drained.

"I have not," Akos said. "Sir."

Malan snapped his book shut and set it on the low table beside him. "Oh, come now, Vakrez." He stood. As ever, he was a stark contrast to his husband: short and thin, his shirt hanging loose instead of tucked, his beard coming in after a few days neglect. "It's a simple request."

"He'll fail," Vakrez said stiffly, his dark eyes fixed on Akos.

Akos stood a little straighter under his scrutiny. He was a bit scrawny, still, thanks to never quite getting enough food at meals, but his soft middle had given way to wiry muscle since he started training with the army. At first, he had been too haunted by his father's death to learn much of anything, but the haze of grief had burned away in time, and only determination had been left. He had to prove himself. He had to become someone the Shotet respected. And then he would be able to find a way to save his brother.

He had no hope of saving himself. His life was already forfeited, thanks to his fate: *The third child of the family Kereseth will die in service to the family Noavek.* His destiny was servitude and death. But his brother Eijeh's wasn't set yet, and Akos was determined that Eijeh wouldn't live out the rest of his life in Shotet.

"And if he fails, so what?" Malan nodded to Akos. "You prove a Thuvhesit isn't fit to wear our armor. And if he succeeds, it reflects well on your training. Either way, the gain is yours, Commander."

Vakrez's head tilted as he considered this. Akos stood still, careful not to fidget. Vakrez didn't like it when he fidgeted. *Focus, Kereseth! Stand up straight, Kereseth! Control yourself, Kereseth!* Akos's life had become a series of demands he couldn't seem to meet.

"Fine," Vakrez said. "I'll arrange for it. Better hope you don't die, Kereseth. It would be an ugly end."

Malan winked at Akos. Akos wasn't sure why Malan had helped him, except that he seemed to have a soft spot for anyone who wasn't at ease in the soldier camp. After all, he was one of the only people there who wasn't a soldier himself.

"I don't need to hope, sir," Akos said.

Vakrez let out a short laugh.

"Heard we should get the funeral pyre ready for you, Kereseth."

A pair of boots with the name Dony written across the toe came to rest in front of Akos. He was sitting cross-legged on the ground near the long, low buildings of the soldier camp, cleaning the practice weapons. The golden grass beneath him scratched at his legs even through his pants, and a beetle buzzed past his ear as he rubbed the cloth along the blade.

He got stuck with a lot of menial tasks the other soldiers didn't have to do, thanks to his status as a prisoner. Taking out laundry and cleaning weapons and repairing practice dummies—it made it impossible for the others to see him as a peer, which was probably the goal.

But it was good for his hands to be busy. It kept him from thinking too much about Eijeh, and what was happening to him in Ryzek's house.

Akos saw two more sets of boots behind Dony, and tensed. It was never good when groups of soldiers came up to him while he was working. Usually it meant he was about to get smacked around.

"You worried about me, Dony?" Akos said, keeping his eyes on his work. "How sweet of you."

"Worried?" Dony scoffed. "I'm excited. We'll probably get to have a party. Funeral rites being what they are."

"I already claimed your bed," one of the others said. "Closer to the window, and all."

"We're probably the same shoe size, right, Kereseth?" the third asked, sticking out his boot in a show of examining it. "Mind if I yank those boots off your body before they burn it?"

Akos was considering his options. He didn't stand a chance against all three of them. Numbers aside, they were all stronger and faster than he was.

As Akos was resigning himself to getting beat up, Dony

looked across the lawn and stiffened.

"Shit," he said. "Commander's headed right toward us."

Akos had never been so relieved to see Vakrez Noavek. He set the practice sword down and tucked the cloth into his pocket. Sweat trailed down the back of his neck. He tried to stand at attention, like the others were, but Vakrez always made him feel like he was slouching.

The commander was broad and muscular, and his posture often forced the buttons on his shirt to strain a little. He wore his own earned armor, distinct because of its perfect, dark plates, unmarred by blades. Nothing was hard enough to damage Shotet armor.

"Your witnesses will be here tomorrow, Kereseth, so ready yourself," Vakrez said.

"Tomorrow, sir?" Akos said.

"I saw no reason to delay. I assumed, based on your eagerness, that you were ready." There was a challenge in Vakrez's eyes. Akos tried to meet it.

"I am, sir," Akos said.

"Then you know participants are permitted to bring one weapon to the rite," Vakrez said. "I've decided to let you borrow one, to make things fair. What would you like?"

"I have what I need already, Commander," Akos replied.

Vakrez's expression was curious. But all he said was, "I expect you to be ready at dawn, then. Dony, I'm making you personally responsible for Kereseth's well-being until then. He'd better show up to his rite in fighting shape and on time."

"Yes, sir," Dony said.

Akos didn't sleep. He didn't really expect to. Instead he went to the kitchens—where he was sometimes sent to peel mezzit roots or wash dishes—and took out the leather packet he kept under his pillow. He stood at the wide wooden counter where the cook sliced meat, and unrolled the leather.

Inside it was a small knife and a dried currentflower. It was whole, with some of the stem still attached to it, though shriveled now from drying. Even dried, the currentflower was more dangerous than any other plant in the galaxy—to anyone but him, that was. His currentgift made him resistant to its power. He had cut it last season, after he killed Kalmev Radix, in the few minutes before Vas's men found him and beat him senseless. And he had saved it since then, knowing it would be useful, even if he didn't know how.

He walked the perimeter of the kitchen. Along each wall was a countertop like the one that held the currentflower, and along the wall, atop each counter, a line of small wooden boxes marked with Shotet characters he couldn't read. So he opened each box instead, sniffing the contents if he couldn't identify them on sight, until he found what he needed.

Then he set water to boiling, and started to brew a poison.

Akos was so nervous by the time dawn came around that he couldn't even look his witnesses in the eye. There were, as the rite required, three of them. Two women and one *sema*, a person who was neither man nor woman. All three wore their own armor—they were supposed to be familiar with the rite, having gone through it themselves. The commander stood with them, trading quiet conversation, when Akos arrived.

They were in the main arena, right in the middle of all the barracks, where most training happened. When Akos first got to the camp, the lieutenant had made him run so many laps around that arena that he had dreamed in laps for weeks.

When a Shotet citizen did the Rite of Armor, a crowd gathered, people played music, someone gave a speech to rally them. But for Akos, it was just the three witnesses and hints of sunlight along the horizon.

The commander waved, and a sight drifted over with a hum and a buzz. "This will be recording your movements live for us to see. If you try to flee across the Divide, we will come find you and kill you. So don't try to flee."

Akos didn't intend to flee. Not without his brother. But he didn't respond. He just faced the horizon and started to run.

The sight buzzed above his head at first, and then moved up, so he almost forgot it was following him. He kept his pace slow but steady, and his breaths even. Stretching in every direction was the low, golden grass between the Divide and the city of Voa, where Akos and Eijeh had first been taken to meet Ryzek, and to hear their fates. Growing among the grasses were small, fragile flowers, some blue, some purple, and occasionally, a rare orange blossom. Akos resisted the urge to stop when he spotted those. He had to stay focused.

All he had to do was put some distance between himself and the soldier camp, and then he might be able to find an Armored One. They looked for remote areas to chew grass.

They didn't really eat it for nutrition, they just chewed it. None of the soldiers Akos had asked really understood why. In fact, nobody really seemed to know much about the Armored Ones, despite their reverence for them.

When he couldn't see the soldier camp behind him anymore, he slowed to a walk and looked for water. He was breathless and sweaty, so he would need it soon, and besides, the Armored Ones drank water, like every living thing, so if he found it, he might find one.

He kept the soldier camp behind him so he wouldn't start wandering in circles. It would be easy to do, here. Everywhere he looked was the same grass, knee-high, soft as hair to the touch. It was dizzying.

Finally he stumbled across a brook. It was the blue flowers that tipped him off—they were growing in clusters, close

to the water. He knelt beside the little stream and rinsed his hands in it, splashed water on his neck to cool himself, then drank from it. He sat back to check his pocket for the vial of poison he had made the night before, then leaned forward to wash his face.

Akos closed his eyes, just for a moment, his head throbbing. He needed to find an Armored One soon, or he would get too tired from sleep deprivation to focus. And he couldn't fail now—couldn't creep back to the soldier camp with his head down, showing them he was just as useless as they thought he was.

He opened his eyes, spotted movement in the grasses to his left, and froze. Clicking seemed to reach his ears from every direction as a dark shape crept closer. He turned to look, just a little, and there it was. An Armored One.

It was such a massive creature that its nearly silent movement defied logic. It made a slippery, whispery sound in the grass, its many legs picking along with surprising care. The clicking came from its pincers, tapping together in front of its broad mouth. It was dark in color, bluish, except for the bright white of its teeth. There were layers and layers of them, each of them a needle as long as his fingers.

And it was *right there*.

When he had imagined this moment, he had seen the Armored One from a distance, and crept closer, trusting his stealth and patience. He would watch it, figure out how and what it ate. Then he would lace its food with poison and wait for it to eat.

That was not what was happening now. The thing was slipping through the grass toward him, its mouth open in a display of jagged incisors, and its bent legs were taller than Akos was when standing. Except he was on his knees. With no weapon except a vial of poison.

Shit.

Akos was so still, his legs were cramping. He spoke the word of calm into his mind, and it did nothing to relax him, nothing to calm the frantic beating of his heart. It was only moments until the thing attacked him, he was sure of it. The soldiers had told him that if he got close enough to an Armored One, it would go into a frenzy and charge, and would not stop charging until he was dead.

It crept still closer. Akos didn't want to die on his knees. It was better to die running—better to die *trying*, at least. So he stood and fled, sprinting across the brook and into the grass, his legs pumping fast, listening, waiting—

But nothing was happening.

Akos looked over his shoulder. The Armored One was still by the brook. It had bent its head to drink from the water. It didn't seem to know he existed, in fact.

Odd.

He stopped running, and turned back toward it. He didn't want to lose this opportunity—it could be hours before he found another one, and he would not be any more alert then than he was now.

He walked toward it, ready to turn and run again if it started to charge. Even his heavier footsteps didn't seem to bother it, so he came closer. He stepped across the brook, to where he had been kneeling before, and kept walking. Step after step, until he was right beside it, within arm's length of its vicious teeth.

It lifted its head—it seemed aware of him, at least, but it wasn't going to attack him.

Akos raised a trembling hand, and touched it to one of the hard plates on the Armored One's side.

The Armored One leaned *in*, pressing into his hand. The clicking of its pincers stopped, and its shiny eyes closed.

"Is it my currentgift?" he asked it. It was the only thing he could think of that would make him different from all the soldiers who had died doing this rite.

"You don't like the current," he said. "Do you want to know something? Neither do I."

The current reminded him that there was something wrong with him. The Thuvhesit destined to betray Thuvhe. The prisoner who wasn't really a Shotet soldier. The only person he had ever heard of who couldn't feel the hum-buzz of the current.

The Armored One blinked at him, almost like it understood him. Akos moved away from it, and it shadowed his movements, taking a small step with him.

Then Akos knew what to do, so the Shotet would remember that he wasn't some fragile thing good only for washing dishes and dying for the Noaveks.

He would lead it back to the soldier camp alive.

Akos Kereseth's hand was outstretched, pressed lightly to the Armored One's side, when he walked it back into the soldier camp in late morning. The witnesses were already there—they'd been watching footage from the sight, so they knew he was coming. But the other soldiers were out, too, dirtying the practice swords Akos had cleaned the day before.

At first, nobody seemed to notice he was coming. But the Armored One was too big to ignore for long. Akos watched all movement stop. Some soldiers bolted for the barracks, as if a thin wooden door would keep them safe from a rampaging Armored One. Akos had heard rumors that they could chew

right through a stone wall if they were riled up enough.

The rest went still, the way he had, next to the brook.

He led the Armored One to the middle of the main arena, and stopped. He knew that if he lifted his hand, the current flowing through all the other soldiers would drive it mad, and it would kill as many of them as it could reach—which might be half the people there. He had never had any power among them, so the feeling that most of their lives rested on the skin touching the Armored One's side was a heady one.

The commander seemed to understand the situation, because he showed Akos his palms, placating.

"Kereseth," Vakrez said. "What are you doing?"

"The rite, sir," Akos said.

"The rite involves the *death* of an Armored One," Vakrez said.

"I know," Akos replied quietly. "But I could decide not to kill it. I could take my hand away and let it devour you." He tilted his head. "I killed a man like you before. I could do it again. And the chaos after might be enough for me to escape, and go home. The feathergrass doesn't affect me, so it would be only two days' journey, on foot."

"You could do that," Vakrez acknowledged, nodding.

"I won't, though," Akos said. He felt like he was finally standing straight. "And it's not because of some hidden Thuvhesit morality, because I don't have that—not when it comes to Noaveks like you." He felt the acid of anger, that pool that never quite dried up, bubbling inside him. "It's because you're going to treat me as a soldier, going forward, and not as a prisoner."

The commander looked him over, just for a tick or two. Then he said, "I don't respond well to threats, Kereseth."

"It's not a threat," Akos said. "I just told you I'm not going to let this thing kill you. But the fact that I could, and I'm choosing not to, means I'm deciding to stay here. Which means I am owed the same respect as the other people in this camp. I know you to be a fair man, and I'm trusting that you'll see that."

Vakrez's eyes were on his, dark and focused. He nodded.

"Finish it," he said.

Akos had dreaded this moment on his walk back to the camp. This creature was innocent. It lived in a world that tormented it constantly with the current. And he had taken advantage of its trust in him. He had used his currentgift against it. It didn't deserve to die.

But Akos knew his own despair. The way hopelessness claimed him on nights he wasn't quite exhausted enough to fall asleep. He was trapped here, held hostage by his own devotion to his brother. He would never see his home again.

He needed to do this.

He reached into his pocket and took out the vial of poison. He pulled the wax seal out of the vial with his teeth, and spit it on the ground. The Armored One's mouth was open wide enough for him to fit his hand in past the first few layers of teeth. He tipped the vial over, pouring the poison into the Armored One's mouth, and he saw the shifting of plates as it swallowed.

Then he kept his palm pressed to its side, so it was soothed by his currentgift while it died.

Vakrez granted him a reprieve for the rest of the day, telling him to get some rest. Akos had worried that basically threatening to kill the commander would make him even crueler, but it had had the opposite effect. If anything, Vakrez seemed to understand him now.

Akos didn't go to his bunk to rest. He went to the long, low building that housed the health clinic. He had been taken there when he first arrived, so a doctor could make sure the long gash under his jaw—courtesy of Ryzek, a reward for his attempt to fight back—was healing properly. He hadn't gone back since then, though he'd been injured multiple times. He didn't like the smell of antiseptic.

The walls of the clinic were raw stone, like the other structures in the soldier camp, but the floors were wood planks instead of packed earth, for sanitary reasons, he assumed. The place was empty except for the nurse, a lean man with a shaved head and a currentblade at his side. Nurses in Shotet were a lot different from nurses in Thuvhe. Everyone Akos came across seemed to be a warrior, here.

"Do you need something?" the man asked.

"I need . . . *vezyel.*" The word for the act came to Akos without much delay, one of the peculiarities of the so-called revelatory tongue. Sometimes he knew words without really knowing them. "Please."

The nurse frowned, but went over to the cabinets on the far wall and took out a little white packet. Akos tore it open, and found a sterile blade, an antiseptic-soaked square of fabric, a vial of ink, and a bandage. He sat down on the edge of one of the beds.

"Do you need help?" the nurse said. "I know you've never done this yourself."

"It's a tattoo, just broken down into parts," Akos said. "I can do it."

He wiped his left arm with the antiseptic, right next to the first mark, which was jagged, an act of violence committed by one of Kalmev's friends. It was on the outside of his wrist, close to the vein that bulged from the back of his hand.

He took the sterile blade and pressed it into his skin. It was more difficult than he thought, to cut himself intentionally. But he pushed himself through the pain, bringing tears to his eyes as he drew the line into his skin.

He took the ink and, using the point of the blade, applied it to the cut. The bite of it was harsh, but not unbearable.

Then he wrapped the bandage around the mark he had made, slumped forward over his knees, and wept.

He now knew something he wished he didn't know:

When it came down to it, he could kill. And not just to save his own life, or to save his brother's life—but to get something he needed. No—to get something he *wanted.*

He would do it again, he was sure, before his time in Shotet was done.

He was ready.

THE

TRANSFORMATIONIST

"Come," she said, and he obeyed.

Together they drove to the outskirts of the city, to a dusty field and the edge of a cliff. The sheer face of rock was dark in color, almost black. The wind blew steady and harsh, and the gray particles from the Zoldan grasses soon coated his clothes like he had rolled in a pit of ash.

She had led him to the edge of the cliff, and he feared that she would push him over. She didn't. She crouched, so he crouched beside her. She pointed down at the birds that roosted among the rocks.

"Their name?" she said to him.

"Calamitas," he answered. They were squat, white birds when fresh born, easy prey if they wandered from the hazardous place where they roosted.

"Yes," she said. "They begin life as weak as we do. Their skulls partially formed, their flesh fragile. The only thing about them that is strong is their beak, harder than stone." She held out a hand to show him a V-shaped scar between her thumb and forefinger. "I was pecked by one, as a child. The force of the impact shattered my hand. It took several surgeries to repair. My father told the doctors to ensure that I scarred, so that I would not forget."

He had not met his grandfather, the man of whom she spoke. But he had seen photographs of him, dark-haired and so pale of eye he looked to have only a pupil, no iris. She looked just like him. He did not like to meet her eyes, but he forced himself to, so that she would not box his ears for his weakness.

She continued, "They use those beaks to tunnel into the cliff face, and when they reach adolescence and the weather cools, they wriggle into the tunnel they have created, if they have survived that long."

His legs ached from crouching, so he tipped his knees forward. Small pebbles dug into his kneecaps, and the wind screamed in his ears.

She lay flat on her stomach, and reached over the edge of the cliff, searching the rock with her hand. When she found it, she clicked her tongue and shifted forward, plunging her arm into a cavity in the rock. She pulled out what looked like a ball of yarn. It was larger than her fist, and white.

She dug her fingers into it, and tore at the woven-looking outside to show him what was inside it. It oozed purple-red, but there were chunky pieces, too, and flashes of beige. She pulled one of the beige things free, and showed him something spiny, with a delicate arch. It was a spine.

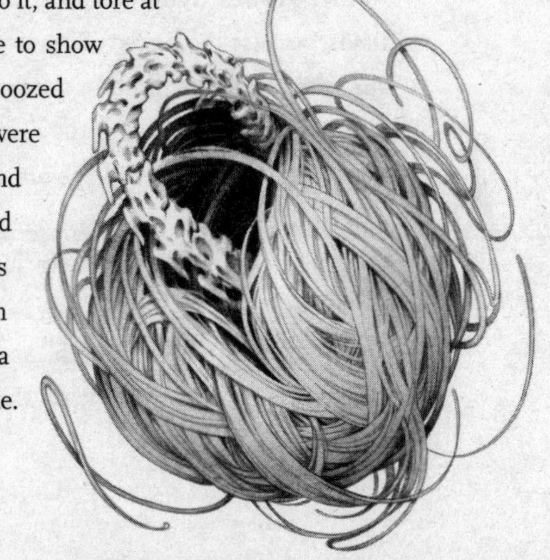

He wanted to vomit. But he didn't.

"They create this sac by biting at their own flesh," she said, holding the spine closer to her face so she could examine it. "Essentially creating a shell for themselves as they transform into their adult forms. The strange thing is, if you bite off your own skin to make a shell, you essentially liquefy yourself."

"So that—" He nodded to the woven thing in her hands. "That's a calamita? Alive?"

"Yes," she said. "Or it was, until I ripped out its spine. But it would have emerged an adult. And you know what adult calamitas look like, don't you?"

He knew. They were small birds, with vicious talons. Their feathers were as hard and sharp as shale. Children were warned against trying to collect the feathers that fell in the fields, because the jagged edges would cut them. They ate the small creatures that lived in the grass, but often killed larger animals for sport, leaving the carcasses where they fell. Or they fought each other in the air, ramming together repeatedly until one broke apart.

Strong, fierce birds they were, calamitas.

He nodded.

"We admire their strength, as adults, and pity them, as children, but do not reflect on the change." She seized his shoulders, suddenly, gripping him hard. Her fingers smeared his shirt with viscera. "They cannot refuse to change. Everything is on a clock in this universe; everything must grow to adulthood. And reaching that point is not always pleasant, you see? The calamita knows this. It claims its change by devouring itself."

Do not look away, he thought as her eyes bored into his. Her eyes were the blue-white of early morning. His own were the opposite, so dark they almost looked black, in low light. His father's eyes. Soulful, she called them sometimes, as if it was an insult.

"This is what we fear to admit," she said, and dusted his face with spit, so forcefully did she whisper. "Transformation will destroy you. It will unmake you."

She moved her bloody hands to his head, gripping his skull and yanking him close to her face.

"And here is the true horror," she said. "You must let it."

Otho's uniform itched at the back of his neck, but he didn't lift his hand to scratch. No sudden movements, that was the rule. He was CG Class 7, which meant guards weren't supposed to touch him, for their own safety, in case the currentgift suppressor around his wrist malfunctioned. So instead he got two escorts from the mess instead of one—two sets of eyes to watch every little twitch of his fingers.

He didn't know why he had been summoned, but in ACYR—the Assembly Center for Youth Rehabilitation—there was rarely anything good at the other end of a summons. If it wasn't punishment that awaited him wherever he was going—and there was always a chance of that, as trouble came for everyone, every now and then—it was news. A death in the family was the most likely variety.

Otho didn't have much family left.

He didn't ask the guards flanking him. He didn't scratch his neck. He didn't look around at the empty cell block. He just listened to the squeak of the guards' shoes on the floor—a shiny material, with some spring in it, a Pithar invention—and walked.

They passed through another set of doors, then another cell block, before making it to the visitation rooms. Otho had been to the big one before, to speak to his uncle Auly and his brother, Catho, but he had only ever gone to a private room to speak to his attorney, and Tyzo's next visit was not scheduled for half a season at least, so he was surprised when the guard on his right grunted "Right here" next to one.

Tyzo sat at the white table within, dressed in a lumpy beige sweater, his glasses askew on his nose. He was a nice enough man, a fellow Zoldan, but Otho had never called him anything but "sir."

Tyzo smiled at him when he walked in. Otho waited for the door to close behind him before sitting across from his lawyer at the table. He felt garish in his prison uniform, which was a vibrant green, with a yellow stripe around the chest and back that declared his CG Class 7 status. Everything else in the room was muted: gray walls, white furniture, Tyzo's sweater and warm brown skin.

"Hello, Otho," Tyzo said, in Zoldan. Talking to him was the only time Otho got to speak his native language while in ACYR—the Zoldan language was a dying one, and few in the galaxy spoke it, particularly among young criminals.

"Sir."

"You look a little thin." Tyzo frowned. "Are you getting enough food?"

Otho didn't know what to say to that. Obviously he was receiving "enough" food, or he would be dead. So how much more than survival was required to be "enough"?

"I think so," he replied.

"I suppose it doesn't matter, anyway, because I have some good news for you," Tyzo said. "You could be going home soon."

Otho blinked at him.

"I have almost two seasons left in my sentence," Otho said. "One season, seven months, and twelve days. I get to go back for a week, for the fluency exam, but—"

The Zoldan government's required language testing had been instated when Otho was young. His parents were part of what was called the Egress Generation—a wave of departures from Zold in search of better opportunities on wealthier planets. Fearing the influence of cultures more powerful and attractive than their own, Zold had passed a series of regulations to preserve the nation-planet's culture. Including a mandatory fluency exam for every Zoldan-born citizen once they turned seventeen.

"I see you've been keeping track of time," Tyzo said with a faint laugh. "Yes, I know, that's why I came to deliver the news in person. Someone came forward to speak on your behalf at your last appeal."

"Who?" Otho's first thought was Catho, but no—he would never do that.

"I can't say—the person was not a legal adult."

"I don't understand," Otho said. "I don't know anyone who would . . ." His mouth was dry. He sipped from the glass of water that Tyzo always poured for him—and he never drank from. "I don't know anyone."

"It appears that isn't true," Tyzo said. He was speaking gently again, the way he always did when he thought Otho might be about to lose it. Otho never did.

"What did they say?" Otho also couldn't imagine what information someone could provide that would reduce his sentence so drastically.

"Their testimony, as well as the evidence they brought forward, proved that you acted in self-defense," Tyzo said. Still gentle. Otho hated it.

"Why should that matter?" Otho said. "I'm guilty. I pleaded guilty."

"It matters." Tyzo frowned at him. "We've discussed this before, Otho."

They had. But it was a system of justice Otho couldn't comprehend. Motive, intentionality, forethought—they were things the law of the land considered, he knew, but to him, they were dust.

"The testimony was enough to grant me an extension, but I'll need your corroborating report to secure your release," Tyzo said. "You just have to tell them what happened, and answer their questions honestly. That's all."

Otho hadn't been able to talk at his own trial. The words just hadn't come to him, no matter how many people asked him questions, no matter how often Tyzo told him he couldn't help a client who wouldn't speak on their own behalf.

"I don't . . ." Otho shut his eyes. "I don't think I want to."

"Otho." Tyzo sighed. "You've been here an entire season for a crime you didn't intend to commit. Haven't you punished yourself enough?"

"That's not . . ." *That's not what this is,* he thought, but then, he wasn't sure what it was. So he stopped talking.

"I'm going to recommend that you be sent home for your fluency exam soon," Tyzo said. "Maybe it'll give you a different perspective. You'll have to wear the currentgift suppressor, of course, and the tracker, but otherwise, your behavior here has been exemplary—so all you need to do is take the fluency exam and return within the week."

"Where will I go?" Otho asked.

"Your uncle is your legal guardian."

"Oh." Otho frowned at his hands, folded on the table in front of him. His knuckles were white. "Okay."

Tyzo was giving him a puzzled look. Tyzo often gave him that look. He reached out as if to touch Otho's shoulder, and then appeared to think better of it, because he pulled his hand back.

"Think about it, okay?" he said, and Otho said that he would, though he wasn't sure why thinking about it in Zold would lead him to a different conclusion.

Tyzo gathered his stack of papers—he always had a stack of papers, though Otho rarely saw him look at them—and left the room. His shoes, too, squeaked. Otho, like every other prisoner in ACYR, had to wear soft slippers. Shoes were weapons, after all. As were belts, hardcover books, butter knives—a long list of things he had not touched in more than a season.

He stayed sitting there until he finished his glass of water.

He didn't fit into the clothes he had worn when he came in. He had grown taller and broader since then. According to the staff member discharging him, it happened all the time. She escorted him to a small closet packed with other people's clothes, and told him to take whatever he wanted. Otho searched out something warm—a worn gray sweater that wasn't too scratchy, and a pair of heavy, loose pants that he had to strap to his waist with a belt. He chose tattered shoes with soft soles, and pieced together a pair of mismatched socks. His old underwear would have to do—he didn't like the thought of wearing someone else's underwear.

Then he had signed some paper and gotten on the transport ACYR had scheduled for him. It was a public Assembly craft that shuttled people from Assembly Headquarters to Pitha and Zold, stopping at ACYR and a fueling outpost in between.

There were government workers on the shuttle already when Otho sat down, chattering in loud voices about trade policy.

Otho chose a seat by one of the long windows, and soon fell asleep with his head against the glass. He had been watching the stars.

"Want some, kid?" one of the Assembly workers asked him in Othyrian. Was it the question that had woken him, or something else? Otho straightened, massaging the crick in his neck.

The man was offering him a bowl of Othyrian fruit. He must have purchased it at the fueling outpost, when they stopped. Otho had stayed on the shuttle, not sure what ACYR rules would say about the journey to Zold. Otho was fiercely hungry, but he shook his head.

"No, thank you," he said.

He was glad that he had woken up, though, because he recognized the planet up ahead, the swirls of color unique to Zold. It was the size of a marble, now, but it would soon swell to fill the entire window, and he would be able to identify cities.

He had told himself that he didn't miss his home, that the things he had loved about it were gone, or not as important as the ones he had lost. But as Zold grew larger in his sights, and he could see the ridges of mountains, the swaths of gray fields, the huge stretches of oceans that defined its surface, he knew he had only been lying to himself. After a season of seeing only the drift of space through the windows of ACYR, the sight of Zold brought tears to his eyes.

He was going home.

A hand touched his shoulder, and he woke to the kind eyes of his uncle. Dazed, he looked around. In the night he had crawled from his bed to the heater in the corner of his room, and he had fallen asleep curled around it, on the floor.

"Breakfast is on the table," his uncle said.

He had landed late last night, and Auly had been waiting for him at the shuttle station. They had paid for a ride back to the city, to an apartment, where Auly had showed Otho a narrow sunroom with glass that was cloudy at the bottom. There was a bed, a low dresser, and a narrow desk. All Otho's, Auly had said, and he made Otho a sandwich before going to bed.

Otho nodded and stood. Auly was a short, sturdy man who wore a visaug—vision augment—on his right eye, to compensate for colorblindness, a common problem among Zoldans.

"I took in a pair of Catho's pants at the waist," Auly said. "They should fit you better now. They're on your chest of drawers."

"Thank you," Otho said. He still couldn't think of the chest of drawers as his, or anything in this apartment. There was only one bathroom, and it smelled of Auly's aftershave. This felt like a temporary place. For Catho, sleeping on the living room couch, it was. He would leave as soon as he had saved enough money for a few months' rent.

"Was it cold out here? I could turn up the heat," Auly said, nodding to the heater.

"No, sir," Otho said. He didn't know how to explain himself, so he didn't try. And he didn't take back the "sir," either.

"Okay," Auly said.

Otho found the pants on the chest of drawers, and carried them, along with his other clothes, into the little bathroom for his shower. He washed quickly, not used to warm water lasting long enough for leisure, and then stood beneath the spray, once he realized that he could. When his skin was flushed and hot, he got out and dressed. Auly had done well with the pants. They were long enough for him—he and Catho were of a height now—but they didn't need a belt anymore.

He had made sure to put on a sweater. One of Auly's old ones. Aunt Juni had knitted it, Auly said, which was why it was lumpy in some places, but the pattern of the weaving was nice and subtle, and it was warm. There were a few small holes in it, but he didn't mind.

Catho was already sitting at the table with Auly when he went in. He didn't look up from the news feed, playing across the screen in his hand. Catho did not indulge in many frivolous objects, but the screen was one he had permitted himself.

He had been awake when Otho returned the night before, but already grabbing his jacket from the hook by the door, on his way out. He had looked Otho over, jaw tight, and said, *You look even less like her than you used to.* And left.

And Otho's hopes that Catho had been the one to speak for him at his hearing—flimsy though they had been—were dashed.

Now, Otho sat eating his breakfast: a portion of synthetic eggs on his plate, piled on a piece of toast. The texture of the eggs was like bits of rubber, and the bread had no flavor, but he ate.

"How long are you going to be on prison break?" Catho said, still without looking up.

"Catho," Auly said in a warning tone.

"What?"

"That's not—"

"One week," Otho said quietly.

"One week?" Catho snorted. "To take a fluency exam? What is that place, a vacation rental?"

Otho could see Auly's mouth opening and closing from the corner of his eye, but he stayed focused on Catho. He said the only thing he could think of:

"Not exactly."

"He could be out longer than that," Auly said, "if he'll agree to speak on his own behalf."

Catho looked at him then. His eyes were full of pain.

"He won't," Catho said. "Because he knows whatever he could say in his defense would be a lie."

He got up, put his plate in the sink, and left the room.

Otho finished his food, and washed his plate, along with Catho's, and the pan Auly had used to cook the eggs.

Otho startled, a little, at the voice over his right shoulder.

"About Catho . . ."

"I know all about Catho," Otho said. He didn't mean for it to come out sounding sharp, but it did.

Luckily, Auly just smiled a little. "I suppose you do."

It was raining.

It rained often in the northwest continent, and it was

usually a mist that hung in the air, light but constant, like this. Otho stood on the sidewalk and tilted his face up to the spray of water. Someone jostled past him, and he paid them no mind.

The streets in the small city of Aunoch were narrow and winding. The sidewalks that bordered them were crowded with locked cycles, the posts of street signs, and people selling things from narrow, wheeled carts, so he walked right on the road. There were still some grounded vehicles in Aunoch, but most of the traffic was adrift, so there wasn't much danger in walking.

A glance in a shop window told Otho his hair was covered in a layer of tiny droplets, each of them glinting. He ran his hands over his head to settle them, then tied his hair in a knot at the nape of his neck to keep it from dripping on his face.

Aunoch was nestled in the crook of the mountain range, and spilled out toward the ocean. It was a poor city on a poor planet, all its buildings run down, with little beauty to them. The apartments were blocks of windows, featureless and painted in pale colors that were now flaking away. The shops

were narrow, with garish signs in a handful of languages. The city's layout was nonsensical to outsiders, roads ending without warning in some spots, or narrowing abruptly. The homeless and the destitute gathered on street corners, selling paper flowers that disintegrated in the wet.

Otho got more nervous the closer he got to the library. There was a chance he would run into a former classmate today. He might see people he hadn't seen since before—

The library was a harsh, brutal building close enough to the water that the air around it smelled like salt. It bulged at random, like a bunch of stones piled together, so it was difficult for newcomers to find the door. Otho kept his head down as he walked in, though he knew he couldn't hide, not really. He was too tall, and too odd-looking, for hiding, even without the reputation that followed him like a cloud of smoke. He went to the desk just inside the entrance.

"Can I help you?" the woman there asked him without looking up.

"Where do I go to take the fluency exam?" he said. He had practiced the question in his head on the way there.

"I can register you," she said. "Surname?"

"Judacre."

The woman at the desk lifted her head at that, studying his face. Then she turned to the little screen propped up at one corner of her desk and started typing.

"First name Otho?"

"Yes, ma'am."

"In a half hour you'll go up to the second floor, end of the hallway on your right. Near the statue of the library founder, you know it?"

"I know it."

She handed him a slip of paper. He kept his steps measured until he was out of sight, then slipped between the stacks of books to catch his breath. He pulled the lapels of his jacket tighter around his body as a wave of shivers overtook him. He felt harsh wind, like he was still atop that cliff, with the blood of the calamita smeared on his cheeks.

Once he had calmed, he walked out from between the stacks and headed for the staircase. Arranged around it were some study tables with people sitting at them, old and young, stacks of books or papers spread out in front of them. Eyes swiveled to find him, and he fought to keep his hands steady at his sides. He knew some of these faces. Time had robbed them of their softness, the gauntness of adolescence taking over as their bodies stretched into adulthood, but their names still came to him as he passed them. Craush, Tadett, Vadau.

And right next to the door, the last person he had seen before they carted him off to ACYR: Jove Doret.

Their eyes met, just for a moment. Jove's eyes were brown, too, though not as dark as Otho's, warmer and richer. Otho had a sudden, vivid memory of looking back before the patrollers shoved him in the back of the floater, and seeing those eyes staring at him from across the street, from the space between the curtains in the Doret house.

He looked away, and walked up the stairs to his fluency exam.

Before, he had lived in a village by the water called Shretva, just down the road from the library. He found his feet taking him there almost without his say-so after the exam, and so he followed them across the narrow, broken road and up the tree-lined hill to the familiar cluster of houses. They were painted, as before, in an array of colors. Rumor had it the practice had started because so many Zoldans were colorblind they just picked whatever paint was available. But there was something appealing about the array of blues, yellows, and pinks nestled in the thinning forest.

Up near the top of the hill, the houses were closer together, and more run-down. That was where he had lived, in a little green house that stuck out an arm's length farther than the others on that side of the street.

He saw from a distance that it wasn't green anymore, but pale yellow, and the windows were lit up from within. Curtains embroidered in bright colors covered them, so he couldn't peek in. There were cheery fake flowers out on the porch in knee-high vases. A green ball had rolled onto the little patch of grass that made up the lawn. A family lived there.

He looked up, to the tallest house on the street, painted white with black shutters. Jove's house.

Perfectly positioned to see too much. And he had—the curtains fluttering at some of the worst moments of Otho's life.

Otho didn't know what possessed him, but he was marching toward that white house, leaving the fake flowers and the green ball behind him. He was knocking on the door, and waiting. The wind tickled at the back of his neck, making him shiver. He was still damp from the rain earlier.

Jove answered the door, his hair sticking up in the middle like he had just tangled his fingers in it. He was tall, compared to most boys their age, but he wasn't like Otho, who had become too long and too broad all of a sudden, and now looked ungainly no matter how hard he tried to stand up straight and move with purpose. His hands—huge, bulging at the knuckle—shook.

"Hello," Jove said finally.

"It was you," Otho said.

"What?"

"You testified at my appeal," Otho said. "You're underage. You're not one of *them*. It could only be you."

"Not one of *them*—you mean the Transformationists?" Jove stepped onto the porch, holding out placating hands. "Otho, are you all right?"

Otho's teeth chattered a little as he said, "Answer me."

"Yes." Jove dropped his hands. "It was me."

Mist dusted Otho's face. It was getting dark; Auly would expect him home soon, might be angry if he wasn't back for dinner. Otho didn't know and he was reluctant to test it.

"I should have done it sooner," Jove said. He swallowed, hard, which Otho knew because he followed the labored bob of his Adam's apple with his eyes. "I'm sorry I didn't."

"What did you even tell them?" Otho snapped. "I was guilty. I am guilty. There's nothing else to say."

"Why are you angry?" Jove said. He didn't sound frustrated—just sad. Somehow that made it worse.

Otho felt frozen to the bone.

"Never mind," he said. "I'm going. I have to go."

He turned, and he was walking away, resolved never to come back here, never to risk seeing his old house made warm by some new family with its damn fake flowers and—

"I didn't *tell* them anything," Jove said, sounding angry now. He grabbed Otho's arm, pulling him back. "Let me show you."

The hill, the street, the houses, they stayed the same. What he could see of the ocean through the trees was dark and choppy. The wind pulled daudid buds away from their branches and sent them, whirling, into the road. And a young man—too far away now to see his features—limped through them.

He was a head shorter than Otho was now, and his dark curly hair wasn't as long, hanging in his face. His feet were bare, his toes swollen and red from prolonged exposure to the cold, like they might burst. His hands were in his armpits.

"I don't need to see this," Otho said to Jove. "I don't need—"

"I think you do," Jove said.

His young self tripped up the steps to his old front door. The house had been green when this happened, and the porch had been buried in snow, with a path cleared by foot traffic. Otho remembered.

Young Otho fell to his knees.

"Please," he called, smacking the heel of his hand against the door. His voice was weak. He sounded so young. "Let me in, please." A desperate kind of moan, almost more animal than man. He thumped the door again with the heel of his hand. "Mom, please, just let me in, it's been hours. . . ."

A flicker of movement. A face in the window beside the door, strict nose, graying hair pulled back tightly, eyes bright as sky. Otho's mother.

Older Otho gasped at the sight of her, but not with pain, and not with guilt—with fear.

He was still afraid of her.

She stared down at her young son through the window. For a moment, it looked as if she might undo the bolt keeping him out. But then she turned and walked away from the glass.

Young Otho slammed his hands against the door again. "Let me in!"

And again. "Please, Mom!"

He bent his head, and sobbed.

And then he disappeared completely, leaving only one Otho on the side of the road with Jove's hand on his arm.

"It was so cold that day, we weren't allowed to walk to school," Jove said fiercely. "I didn't know what had happened, for the longest time. I thought maybe you had done something horrible and she had turned you out of the house . . . that maybe you were dangerous or had lost your mind and she was calling the patrols to have them pick you up." Jove's face crumpled. "And then I realized it was—a ritual. That repulsive . . . *cult* . . . That whole 'prove your mettle, survive, transformation through destruction, self-immolate and then come to life again in the flames' Transformationist *bullshit*—"

Transformation will destroy you. It will unmake you.

Otho turned away and began walking down the hill.

Stumbling a little, his feet unsteady, as they had been that day he almost lost them to the frost.

And you must let it.

"Otho!" Jove called, but Otho didn't stop.

God, he so hated to be cold.

Zold was home to all manner of religious ascetics, who eschewed basic comforts in favor of meditation and prayer; or lived simple, unadorned lives; or even ones who wandered to remote areas alone and fasted for long periods, returning dusty and thin and in search of bread.

But there were none quite like the Transformationists. They believed not in emptiness, but in what his mother had called "unmaking." Self-annihilation. Even water, they reasoned, must boil before it is pure.

Do not worship at the altar of comfort, his mother had said. Or your life will be one of waste, and your character unworthy of the kingdom that follows death. She had been their teacher, his and Catho's, their guide, their sanctifier. Responsible for the enduring strength of their immortal souls.

Catho had taken to it more than Otho had. Otho had never learned, always giving in to his weakness too soon. She had to be harder on him, to shape him as she was supposed to. She never laid a hand on him; that would have been too simple, and simple methods brought about simple results. No, she had needed to alter the core of what he was, and to do that required innovation. She had tested him, over and over again, from the moment he was old enough to comprehend her teachings.

And for the last test she would give him, she had noted what he loved as a child: crouching by the fire on cold nights, wrapping himself in blankets, standing in the sun in the heat of summer. And she had used it as a weapon against him, when the time came for him to transition from child to adult. She had forced him into the cold. Survive for one day, she said, and you will become a calamita.

He had lasted six hours.

Otho walked the winding, confusing streets of Aunoch for hours, his thoughts scattered and incoherent. He heard echoes of his own voice begging his mother to let him in, and chills washed over him each time, until his body trembled.

Auly was playing the little instrument in the corner of the living room when Otho returned to the apartment, his fingers dancing over the line of metal tubes and sending out airy notes. It was not a song, exactly, but a mood. He didn't stop when Otho came in, and Otho was glad of it. He stood and listened for a few minutes, his clothes still damp.

Catho came home in the middle of his reverie, throwing his keys on the table by the door and shrugging off his jacket like he was angry with it. Otho didn't have to guess where his anger was really directed.

"I was just at the midweek meeting," Catho said hotly.

Auly's music petered out.

The midweek meeting was only for adult Transformationists, so Otho had never been allowed to attend. All he knew was that his mother had often come back from it in a wild state, full of new ideas that usually meant Otho would suffer some kind of deprivation.

It was no accident that he had grown a head taller in juvenile detention, where there was legally mandated access to regular meals.

"Apparently the Zoldan government is investigating us," Catho said. "And do you know why?"

Otho just stared at his brother.

"Oh, could it be that someone reported one of our sacred

practices as 'criminal misconduct'?" Catho said. "The accused, by the way, was Anisae Judacre."

Ani, their father had called her, when he was still alive. *Ani, tell me a story.* She had always been a good storyteller, with a low, throaty voice and delicate gestures that created shapes in the air.

"It's not enough that you took her from me," Catho all but growled at Otho, his eyes bright with tears. "You had to take her reputation, too? And now, maybe even the only place I've ever belonged, the only people I've ever belonged *to*?"

That it had not been Otho's choice to appeal his sentence, or for Jove to testify about what he had seen, didn't matter, he knew. Otho had taken so much from Catho he had no right to answer, no right even to apologize. Their *mother*. What greater theft was possible?

"What your mother did, or didn't do"—Auly spoke up from the corner where he still sat with his hands on the instrument—"is not your brother's fault, Catho."

"You know nothing about it, Auly," Catho snapped.

"I know enough," Auly said. "I have never asked you to be kind to Otho, or to forgive him, but at the very least, you will leave him alone, or you will leave this apartment."

"Do you even have anything to say?" Catho had turned back to Otho, and he was close to Otho's face, spitting his rage like a cat. "Or are you just going to stand there staring at me?"

Otho's voice was gone, his being pulsing only with wordless feeling.

"We should have her named a prophet," Catho said, quiet now. "She certainly saw into your future."

I fear for you, Otho. I fear you are the kind of soft that will never harden.

Catho grabbed his keys from the table and left the apartment.

Otho met Auly's eyes.

"I want you to know," Auly said, "that I am the one who told your lawyer to appeal your sentence. Whether you testify on your own behalf or not is up to you—but I wanted you to know that I'd like you to."

He lifted his hands from the instrument just high enough to begin again, tapping at the little metal tubes so they sang. Otho listened for a moment, until the feeling returned to his legs, and then went into his little room to change his clothes.

That night, he woke after an hour of sleep, shivering violently, and crawled to the heater to lay in front of it, curled in a ball.

In the morning, there was a heavy blanket on top of him and a pillow clutched in his arms. Auly must have given them to him as he slept.

Otho stood in the sunroom, considering a plant. It was on the desk—a shola bush, a native Zoldan plant that would grow anywhere. It was largely considered a weed, but it bloomed monthly, little blue flowers the color of the sky around the rising moon.

Auly had put it there for him, he was sure. A way of saying

that Otho was here to stay—or could be, if he wanted to be. Which meant that Otho wasn't sure that he wanted to water it, as if watering it would be taken as a sign that he had made some kind of decision.

He had just decided not to water it when a knock came at the door. For a moment he went rigid, remembering. The patrols had knocked on his door, after it happened. But it was over now, he told himself. They would not come again.

He forced himself to open the door. Jove stood in the run-down hallway, by the short row of shoes. He was twisting his fingers together in front of him.

"Hi," Jove said. "Sorry to intrude, I just—"

"Come in," Otho said, holding the door open for him.

Jove looked taken aback, like he had not expected it to be that easy. But he slipped his shoes off and came in.

"I had your uncle's address from the whole appeal thing," Jove explained. "And . . . is that a dadsh?"

He wandered over to the instrument in the corner, and stood over it for a moment, his fingers splayed above it, as if desperate for a song. Then they tapped out a rhythm on the dainty metal, one hand finding a rhythm and the other a melody. It was more of a song than the ambient music Auly had played the night before, but Otho was taken in by it all the same. There had never been much music in his life before.

"My parents were into traditional Zoldan instruments. Well, my dad is dead, but my mom still is," Jove said as he played. "You might say they were the opposite of the Egress

Generation. They stuffed our lives—me and my sister—with everything Zoldan from the moment we could walk. She takes Zoldan folk dance lessons at the community center every week."

"I've never seen Zoldan folk dance," Otho remarked.

"Yeah, I guess the Ts don't go to the Heritage Festival, do they?" Jove lifted a shoulder.

It was strange for Otho to hear them—his former religious community—spoken of so casually as "the Ts." He had never stood outside them before. At ACYR, no one had been Zoldan, so no one had known who they were, and Otho had not been chatty enough to explain them. And before ACYR, he had been swallowed up in them all the time.

"No," he said.

"Sorry, I should probably explain why I'm here," Jove said, stepping away from the instrument. He stuffed his hands in his pockets. "My mom wanted to invite you to dinner. Well—I mean—I wanted to invite you, too. But it's her house."

Otho stared at him.

"You don't have to. Obviously."

"I know," Otho said.

"Yeah, sure." Jove had never looked more uncomfortable in all the time Otho had known him. Which was all his life. They had attended the same school from year one on, always in different orbits, but Otho had noticed him. He had gone through too many awkward phases to be popular with their classmates, but he had an ease about him that meant he always had friends. He was, in many ways, Otho's opposite.

"Okay," Otho said. "I'll go."

Jove smiled, and a dimple appeared in one of his cheeks.

Otho had never been inside Jove's house. He had only seen it from the street as he walked down from the cliffs, the curtains with their warm glow, and, sometimes, he heard raucous laughter coming from inside. They hosted parties for the Heritage Festival, and floaters and grazers swarmed the street those nights, as did people in Zoldan folk costumes, intricately embroidered with native plants and lines of poetry and familiar cityscapes.

He wasn't sure what to expect when he stepped inside. Jove's family was the wealthiest on the street, but that didn't mean they were wealthy by any other standard. At first glance, the living room struck him as the same as any Zoldan living room, cushions stuffed into every corner, a long, low table taking up most of the floor space, books lining the walls. But upon closer inspection, he saw that the table was made of off-world wood, and the fabric of the cushions was woven from natural fibers, not synthetic.

There was a pile of wood shavings on the table, with a carving knife beside it, and a piece of delicate wood curled into a flower. Otho was leaning in to look at it when he heard laughter from somewhere deeper in the house, and he remembered to follow Jove to the kitchen.

"Mom, this is Otho," Jove said to the woman at the stove. She was small and trim, with black hair like Jove's, and had a towel tossed over her shoulder. At Otho's name, she looked up with a smile that was distinctly lopsided and forced a deep dimple into one of her cheeks.

"Hi, Otho," she said. "I would shake your hand, but I have grease all over my fingers."

"Um, hello? I, too, exist." A small voice spoke from the corner of the room. A girl—not as small as her voice, though she couldn't have been older than twelve—sat at the table on the other side of the room, a book propped up in front of her.

"Sorry, Dash, I thought you were deep in it," Jove said. "Otho, this is Dasha, also known as Dash."

"It's a pleasure to meet you both," Otho said.

"Ooh, is he fancy?" Dash said.

"No, he just has good manners." Jove's mom—who, Otho now remembered, was named Kiiva—jabbed the wooden spoon she was using to stir sauce at her daughter. "Take notes."

"It figures you'd immediately like Jove's boyfriend more than me," Dash said.

The back of Otho's neck warmed, and he knew he was likely getting splotchy, the way he often did when embarrassed. Not his favorite quality about himself.

"Dasha!" Jove grabbed a dish towel and threw it at Dasha, who cackled and used her book as a shield.

"Sorry," Jove mumbled at Otho a moment later. He added, "Siblings," with a sigh, as if it explained something. "Come on, I'll give you the tour."

He showed Otho the bathroom—"You're a guest, so you can use the little sparkly soap if you're into that"—and pointed out Dasha's bedroom, and his mother's, before opening the door to a narrow passage with glass walls that led to his own room.

"It used to be a greenhouse," he said, "and my parents just put up a curtain and called it good."

All the walls of Jove's room were glass. He walked the perimeter when they entered, drawing navy blue curtains across each wall. There was a bed wedged in one corner, but dominating the space was a desk with musical instruments arranged around it. Some of them were traditional ones, like the dadsh Otho's uncle had, and some were unfamiliar, like a waterfall of iridescent discs that, when touched, sounded like rain.

"Pithar," Jove said. "I found it at a resale place in the Shabby District. It was a little busted, but turns out replacing the discs isn't that hard if you're determined and possess very small pliers."

"You make music," Otho said. A moment later, he felt stupid, because *could you have made a more obvious observation*?

"Want to hear?" Jove said a little tentatively.

"Yes, I do," Otho said.

Jove grinned. "You're very direct."

Otho wasn't sure what to say to that.

"That was a compliment," Jove said, squeezing both eyes shut. He opened one, just a crack. "Sorry. Please, sit. I'll queue it up."

Otho sat in the chair, and Jove leaned in to tap on the screen set up on his desk. His head was right over Otho's shoulder, and Otho made the mistake of turning to look at patchy stubble on his jaw and clear brown skin.

Jove picked up the earspeaks on the desktop and slipped one into Otho's right ear, keeping the left one for himself. A moment later sound spilled into Otho's head in the form of a buzzing beat. Layered over it was low keening, like a voice, but too reedy to be a person. The pace picked up, and new instruments filled all the spaces in Otho's mind, whispering tones and rapid, upbeat notes with rich underpinnings.

It was different from listening to Auly tinker with the dadsh, though Otho had liked that well enough. This music reached deep inside Otho and yanked something loose. The hair on his arms stood on end, and he blinked, hard, to get rid of tears before Jove noticed them. It wasn't normal to react this way to music, he knew—so either Jove was remarkable, or there was something wrong with Otho, or maybe both.

"You like it?" Jove asked after a moment.

Otho swallowed, hard, and nodded. Jove turned off the music, and Otho felt the absence of it. Silence swelled between them, suddenly taking up all the space.

"We didn't listen to music," he said.

"Never?"

Otho shook his head.

"I guess I should have realized. Ascetics, and all," Jove said, and then, softly, he asked, "Did you . . . like it? Growing up a T?"

"I . . . no," Otho said. Everything in their house had been practical. No wood carvings intended just to be beautiful. No music. No laughter coming from the kitchen. He shivered a little. "I don't think I want to talk about it anymore."

"Okay," Jove said. He straightened, and said, "We'd better head back to the kitchen, or Dasha's going to become insufferable."

"Dash, I'm only asking for thirty minutes of your time, really." Kiiva plucked the book out of Dasha's hands and set it on the counter. "Make it quality, please."

They were sitting at the kitchen table, which Otho had helped Jove set with red and white dishes. They were eating auride, a dish made of chunks of root vegetables covered in a tart vinegar sauce, eaten with bread. Otho took care to sit up straight and take small bites, so he didn't make a mess. He wondered how aware Jove's mother was that he had come from ACYR, and hadn't used a knife in an entire season.

Dasha sighed dramatically, robbed of her book, and turned her attention to her plate.

"Tell me about your class today," Kiiva said to Dasha.

"The music," Dash said, rolling her eyes, "was *terrible*. This weird plinky-plunky stuff from Thuvhe."

As it turned out, Dasha was a dancer—not just the Zoldan traditional dance that Jove had told Otho about earlier, but a variety of styles, and every day of the week brought another class or practice or performance.

As she spoke about her class, she gestured, and transformed, somehow—her too-long, too-thin limbs becoming graceful and purposeful. Dasha was more herself when in motion.

Kiiva, meanwhile, was the opposite. She went still when

other people spoke, and focused in, forgetting her food and tilting her head toward Dasha. Otho's mother had been focused, too, but not on listening, and so the effect of the expression was different. Otho wondered what it was like, to be listened to like that all the time. He wondered if Jove knew that his experience was singular.

Otho cleaned his plate, finishing long before anyone else did, and listened as Jove asked about specific people in Dasha's class—"Is she still mad at you for the toe-stomping incident?" "No, once her toenail grew back she was fine"—and watched Kiiva change the tilt of her head, the set of her eyebrows.

But soon enough, Kiiva's unrivaled focus was on *him.*

"How is your brother, Otho?" she asked. "Now that you've moved, I don't see him as often."

There were a dozen answers that would have done the job. *He's fine, he seems to be all right, he's working, we don't talk much.* But Kiiva's stare was intent and her question careful, and Otho forgot to guard himself with silence.

"He hates me," Otho said softly.

Kiiva's mouth tugged down at the corners.

"I don't blame him," Otho said. He couldn't look away. "But now I'm alone."

"I'm sorry," Kiiva said to him. She stretched out a hand and rested it on top of his, gently. "I can't imagine where you've been."

Otho tried not to think about the season he had spent at ACYR, or the months before it, ramping up to his final test. And that moment, the worst moment, the sudden flaring of his currentgift as it focused on his mother with unimaginable strength.

Otho pushed back from the table with a shudder.

"Thank you for dinner," Otho said. "I have to go. I'm sorry."

"Are you all right, dear?" Kiiva asked, frowning. Jove was on his feet, reaching; Otho brushed past him and walked out of the house and into the snow—

But there was no snow, it was almost summer, and the air was thick with humidity. Still Otho shivered, and went out to the street, turning right instead of left, to make the climb to the top of the hill, where the calamitas bred and burrowed and matured.

His feet had been numb when he walked this path that winter, and he had fallen every few feet on the packed snow, catching himself on hands tucked into sleeves. He had not known that his currentgift had summoned her from their little house, not even giving her the option of grabbing her coat, so she went out into the snow in just a dress and slippers.

He could still hear the footsteps behind him.

Otho reached the top of the hill, where the land spread out flat before him, before abruptly ending at the edge of the cliff. Shining above were Zold's two swollen moons, one lower than the other and to its right, like a child holding a mother's hand.

He walked closer to the edge, and heard a voice on the wind.

"Otho!" It was Jove.

He turned. Jove was pulling his jacket tight across his chest, his wild black hair tossed up by the wind.

"Your family . . ." Otho laughed a little. "Your house . . .

your *life*, it's . . ." He shook his head, the words leaving him. "I didn't know life could be like that."

Jove had come close enough that he didn't have to shout. He stood at Otho's shoulder, close enough to touch but not touching, so they were both staring at the cliff's edge.

Otho's lips felt numb. "It happened here, you know."

The snow had come up past her bony ankles and soaked through her slippers.

"My currentgift made her follow me up here," he said. "I didn't know I could do that. It made her want to . . . want to come out into the cold, where I was." He tilted his head. "Why didn't it make her want to let me in the house, instead?"

"I don't know," Jove said softly.

Otho's whole body was shivering now. His teeth chattered before he spoke again. "She came out of its trance when she reached the edge, and then she started yelling at me. Calling me . . . whatever. Nothing new, the same old insults I'd heard a thousand times."

Weak, and *useless*, and *soft*, and *dull*.

"And then—I wanted to be rid of her, I wanted to be free. I watched her go over the edge, and that was the last I saw of her." Otho closed his eyes and tilted his head back, so the twin moons would shine on his face. "I didn't want her to die, I swear, I—"

"I know," Jove said.

They stood in silence for a while, and then Jove spoke again.

"I saw her follow you up. I assumed she was going to bring

you home, make things right. Because that's what parents do. That's what family does."

Otho looked at Jove instead of the cliff. At the faint indent where a dimple would appear, in his cheek, if he smiled. At the dark fringe of eyelashes that blended into his eyebrows when his eyes were wide open.

"It wasn't right, what she did to you," Jove said. "None of it—the name-calling, the cruel tests, none of it."

Otho still wasn't sure he believed that. Maybe he was too far gone, too calamita to understand softness anymore, not calamita enough to fly. But she had told him that a person couldn't refuse to change, and he was sure of that, sure that it was time for him to change.

"Is that why you testified?" Otho asked. The wind died down, making everything sound muffled to him. "Because . . . you thought it was right?"

"No," Jove said. He laughed, and that was when Otho noticed the tears in his eyes. "I like you, Otho. All the odds were against you becoming this person, but here you are, kind, right to the core of you. And you don't deserve to be shut away."

Jove leaned a little closer, so their arms were up against each other.

"You asked me if I liked growing up as one of them," Otho said then. "I didn't. But I thought it would make me strong."

She had told him to endure, that enduring would make him a calamita—hard as rock, sharp as a knife, fierce as a storm. But it hadn't. It hadn't.

"I tried not to want anything, because wanting more than

you had, more than it took to survive, was weakness, and I couldn't be weak." The grass tickled at his ankles, at the gap of skin between socks and pants. "Even now, I'm scared that if I want anything, I'll want everything, and I won't be able to stop."

Jove slid his hand into Otho's, and squeezed.

"You *will*," he said, and it was hushed, a promise and a revelation in his mouth. "You'll want *everything*. You'll ache for things you can't have, and will never have. Impossible things, and improbable things, and stupid things, and evil things—you'll want them all." Jove smiled a little, his cheek dimpling. "But you'll also *get* things. Things you want. And . . . they'll make your life full, and they'll make it so you can keep going, and . . ." He shrugged. "They'll keep you warm."

Otho wanted so badly to be warm again.

He touched Jove's cheek, turning the other boy's head toward his. He leaned in slowly, as if asking for permission, and Jove closed the gap, his lips pressing to Otho's. The wind rushed around them, biting into Otho's skin, but Jove just turned toward him, a warm, strong barrier against the cold.

That night, Otho heard Auly's music the moment the elevator doors opened.

He took his shoes off by the door, and set them next to his uncle's. Catho's still weren't there, and Otho hadn't expected them to be.

He unlocked the door, and Auly nodded a greeting at him. Otho hung up his jacket and stood in the living room, listening to the song.

"You're home late. Did you have a good night?" Auly asked him, his hands still moving across the instrument. Otho nodded.

"Will you call Tyzo tomorrow?" Otho said.

Auly lifted his hands.

"Okay," he said. "What should I tell him?"

"Tell him I'll testify," Otho said.

Auly smiled, and played on.

Otho let his uncle's smile, and the music that floated away from the dadsh, and the memory of Jove huddled against him, fill him and keep him warm.

ACKNOWLEDGMENTS

THANK YOU, THANK YOU, THANK YOU to:

Katherine Tegen, my editor, and Joanna Volpe, my agent, who both encourage me to invent new worlds, explore new ideas, and dream big. You guys keep me afloat. <3

At HarperCollins, Sara Schonfeld in editorial; Aubrey Churchward and Cindy Hamilton in publicity; Bess Braswell, Audrey Diestelkamp, and Nellie Kurtzman in marketing; Andrea Pappenheimer, Kathy Faber, Kerry Moynagh, Kirsten Bowers, Heather Doss, Susan Yaeger, Jessica Abel, Fran Olson, Jennifer Wygand, Deborah Murphy, Jennifer Sheridan, Jessica Malone, and Jessie Elliott in sales; Brenna Franzitta and Christine Corcoran Cox, my copyeditor and proofreader, respectively; Alexandra Rakaczki, Josh Weiss, and Gwen Morton in managing editorial; Nicole Moulaison and Vanessa Nuttry in production; Barbara Fitzsimmons and Amy Ryan in design; and of course Jean McGinley, Suzanne Murphy, and Brian Murray, who keep the whole train on its tracks. Thank you all for your incredibly hard work.

Erin Fitzsimmons, for designing this beautiful book—you've truly outdone yourself. Ashley Mackenzie, the artist who made these pages so amazing—it's been a thrill to see your work take shape.

At New Leaf Literary, Abbie Donoghue, Devin Ross, Jordan Hill, Mia Roman, Veronica Grijalva, Pouya Shahbazian, Hilary Pecheone, Cassandra Baim, Meredith Barnes, Joe Volpe, and Madhuri Venkata—you have all contributed to this book and to my career in different ways, but together you're a goddamn powerhouse of a team. I am so lucky to work alongside you all.

The writers who buoy me personally and professionally behind the scenes, particularly Margaret Stohl, Sarah Enni, Maurene Goo, Kara Thomas, Kate Hart, Laurie Devore, Kaitlin Ward, Amy Lukavics, and Michelle Krys—you ladies routinely inspire me with your talent and make me laugh until I weep. Courtney Summers and Somaiya Daud, who read early versions of these stories—you are the smartest, kindest, dearest, and most ferocious of women, and I think the world of both of you. Alex Bracken, Marie Lu, and Neal Shusterman, all writers I admire deeply, for your early reads of this book—I am so honored. All my YALL and YALL-adjacent people, you are a constant delight.

My parents, Barb and Frank, for being every bit as loving as my characters' parents are not. My family: Ingrid, Karl, Frankie, Dave, Candice, Beth, Roger, Tyler, Rachel, Trevor, Tera, Darby, Andrew, Billie, and Fred, for all the support you give without asking for anything in return. My friends who aren't writers, who get me out of my own head. God bless you.

Nelson, husband and fiercest friend—sometimes I dream about worlds where I didn't find you. They are even worse nightmares than the ones I have about bugs.